As they be[gan walking toward their] rooms, she walked in front of him.

Down the hall toward her door. As though she was just going to go inside, go back to their old lives, without a peep.

He should rejoice at that. In fact, the entire trip back he'd conceived a plan to let it all go. Let it play out. See what she did. See how she handled all this. He'd determined it was the best course of action to simply *let things be*.

She reached her door, lifted a hand to the doorknob, and he couldn't keep the words inside, all his plans ash around him, just like always seemed to happen when it came to her.

"When were you planning on telling me?"

She stopped, her hand frozen on the doorknob. For a moment, she said nothing, keeping her back to him. Stiff. *Caught*. But she did not give in right away. "Telling you what?"

"That you are pregnant."

A sensationally thrilling Harlequin Presents duet from Lorraine Hall.

Babies for Royal Brides

From wedding ring to royal heir!

The royal family of Alis live a fairy-tale existence. At least, they're *supposed* to. But while Crown Prince Alexandre and Princess Evelyne were born into a world of privilege, they grew up under their father's iron rule. Now they're planning to rip up the King's royal rule book! But could two marriages of convenience followed by two pregnancies not just rewrite the kingdom's future, but give Alexandre and Evelyne the chance to experience a love they thought only happened in storybooks?

You're cordially invited to the wedding of...

Evelyne and Gabriel
Secretly Pregnant Princess

Ines and Alexandre
King's Heir Ultimatum

Both available now!

KING'S HEIR ULTIMATUM

LORRAINE HALL

PRESENTS

If you purchased this book without a cover you should be aware that this book is stolen property. It was reported as "unsold and destroyed" to the publisher, and neither the author nor the publisher has received any payment for this "stripped book."

ISBN-13: 978-1-335-21366-2

King's Heir Ultimatum

Copyright © 2026 by Lorraine Hall

Recycling programs for this product may not exist in your area.

All rights reserved. No part of this book may be used or reproduced in any manner whatsoever without written permission.

Without limiting the exclusive rights of any author, contributor or the publisher of this publication, any unauthorized use of this publication to train generative artificial intelligence (AI) technologies is expressly prohibited. Harlequin also exercises their rights under Article 4(3) of the Digital Single Market Directive 2019/790 and expressly reserves this publication from the text and data mining exception.

This is a work of fiction. Names, characters, places and incidents are either the product of the author's imagination or are used fictitiously. Any resemblance to actual persons, living or dead, businesses, companies, events or locales is entirely coincidental.

For questions and comments about the quality of this book, please contact us at CustomerService@Harlequin.com.

TM and ® are trademarks of Harlequin Enterprises ULC.

 Harlequin Enterprises ULC
22 Adelaide St. West, 41st Floor
Toronto, Ontario M5H 4E3, Canada
www.Harlequin.com

HarperCollins Publishers
Macken House, 39/40 Mayor Street Upper,
Dublin 1, D01 C9W8, Ireland
www.HarperCollins.com

Printed in Lithuania

Lorraine Hall is a part-time hermit and full-time writer. She was born with an old soul and her head in the clouds, which, it turns out, is the perfect combination to spend her days creating thunderous alpha heroes and the fierce, determined heroines who win their hearts. She lives in a potentially haunted house with her soulmate and rambunctious band of hermits-in-training. When she's not writing romance, she's reading it.

Books by Lorraine Hall

Harlequin Presents

A Diamond for His Defiant Cinderella
A Wedding Between Enemies
Pregnant, Stolen, Wed
Unwrapping His Forbidden Assistant

The Diamond Club

Italian's Stolen Wife

Rebel Princesses

His Hidden Royal Heirs
Princess Bride Swap

Work Wives to Billionaires' Wives

The Bride Wore Revenge

Babies for Royal Brides

Secretly Pregnant Princess

Visit the Author Profile page at Harlequin.com.

For best friends.

CHAPTER ONE

King Alexandre Enzo Rodrigo Lidia had been a married man for almost a year. He had been king for almost three months, thanks to the untimely death of his father.

He knew far more about how to be a king than about being a husband.

Being a king made sense, after all. There were laws to uphold, the previous king's mistakes to fix and a country to usher into a new era of peace and stability.

Being a *husband* was something else entirely. If he was not royalty, at least. Luckily, he was.

He had not chosen his wife. Ines had been chosen for him. At the time, Alexandre had been rather grateful that his father's choice had been bearable. King Enzo had been a vindictive despot of a king, and even worse as a father, so Enzo had not chosen Ines for anything except access to her father's wealth.

She could have been anything. A pampered, spoiled, dramatic nuisance. A pompous, withdrawn, cruel snob. The terrible options were endless.

But Ines had turned out to be a wonderful princess and an even better queen. She was dutiful, modest and quiet. She was kind and pleasant, but not dull. She never behaved above anyone, and so the country of Alis quite loved her. She was a workhorse and never complained, always happy to take on the next royal task assigned.

If she disagreed with him about anything, they had calm, reasonable discussions, and he could almost always talk her around to his way of thinking.

Alexandre was hardly ever wrong.

He'd had a lifetime of preparing to be king—of preparing to undo every horrible thing his father had enacted. On his mother's deathbed, she had tasked him with fixing everything. Alexandre might have only been five, but he had taken that promise he'd made her quite seriously. For the nearly twenty-five years between her death and his father's three months ago, he had watched his father and planned to fix everything the horrible man had done to his family, to his county.

For the past three months, he had worked exclusively to undo all his father's petty, militaristic whims.

Not that Alexandre was perfect. He could not claim to be. He had failed many in his life. He had not been able to protect his mother from the wrath of his father's so-called love. He had not been able to protect her from the medical complications that had stolen her life at Evelyne's birth. He knew he had not always been able to protect his younger sister from the abuses of their father as she'd grown up.

But he had done his level best. And would continue to do so, until death took him. There was simply no other choice.

So Ines was a better wife than Alexandre could have ever hoped for, taking on her responsibilities so easily, so adeptly. She could connect with their kingdom in a more...*emotional* way than a protector could.

Perhaps the necessary heir had not come as quickly as he might have liked, but that was hardly her fault. And now, he needn't worry about it. Thanks to an old Alis law, the heir did not need to be born from the eldest child or even the male heir. The first child born of the following generation became heir to the throne.

His sister was due any day now, and Evelyne's son would be the future king. So Alexandre no longer needed to worry about producing an heir with Ines. His sister and his best friend had done it for him.

It had been a relief.

Not because it was any trial to bed his wife. Quite the opposite. *That* was the problem. He did not have room for passion or interest or *relationships* in his life. The kind of emotion that marked his parents was the kind that ruined kingdoms.

Alexandre would not stand for it.

Ines was meant to be his wife in name only...once she'd produced an heir. But an heir had not come. Doctors had assured him that there was nothing medically preventing either of them from conceiving a child. The doctor had advised him—and her—to *relax*.

Something Alexandre could only see as the enemy. Because if he *relaxed*, he could make a mistake. One that would harm his entire country. That would have been impossible enough before his father's unlikely death three months ago.

Now? Relaxation would be the same as catastrophic. He had *years* of work yet before he could fully ensure Alis was on the right track.

So the minute Evelyne had returned from her exile after Enzo's death, pregnant with the Alis heir, Alexandre had stopped keeping his weekly...*appointments* with Ines.

They had not discussed it, but she had not mounted any kind of argument or asked him why he no longer came to her bedchamber on the assigned evenings. She let it slide.

This was the beauty of Ines. A good queen let things that did not matter slide.

So he was more than a little surprised to find his wife in his office this morning when he arrived. He glanced at his watch. She was not one to interrupt his daily routine.

"Ah, good morning, Ines. I'm afraid I don't have time to talk just now. I have an appointment." And his concentration was already a bit scattered with the news Evelyne had gone into labor. This information had left him feeling...more on edge than he'd like.

He could remember the day Evelyne had been born more clearly than he liked. The hushed whispers. The screaming. The blood when he'd snuck himself into his mother's room and she'd tasked him with saving the baby she'd birthed, the kingdom she left behind.

"Yes," Ines agreed in the here and now. "I am your appointment." She sat in the chair opposite his desk, dressed for a day of royal meetings. A trim suit in a vibrant blue. Her brown hair with hints of mahogany was pulled back in an elegant twist. She wore an exquisitely simple gold pendant around her neck, blue diamonds at her ears that matched the color of her eyes, and his wedding ring on her finger. Her left hand rested over the right in her lap, her ankles crossed and drawn slightly beneath her chair.

She really was quite perfect. In every picture, in every portrait, in every moment, Ines looked like a queen.

He did not allow himself to consider the rare moments he saw her mussed, her lips swollen from his. Those moments tended to threaten his necessary equilibrium. His required focus.

So he supposed she was *not* perfect. She could stand to be a *little* duller. Perhaps she would not pop into his thoughts unbidden if he did not find her quite so beautiful. But a beautiful queen was something indeed, and to wish her duller was no wish for his kingdom, so he shoved that thought away.

He skirted his desk and took a seat so they were opposite each other. A bit like strangers.

In some ways, she was a stranger to him. He might know that she preferred cream in her coffee, lemon in her tea. He might even know what she looked like beneath her clothes—far too beautiful, small, soft, perfect—and what sounds she made in pleasure—haunting, really. But sometimes it struck him that he did not know *her*.

She kept herself hidden behind a royal mask, just as he did. A good thing, Alexandre knew. A preferred thing. And still...sometimes he'd see her tucked away with Evelyne somewhere, laughing over something, and he'd have the strangest desire to want to know what it was about, what she found funny, what made her smile just like that.

But he did not have time for such things, and she was definitely not laughing this morning. "You've been avoiding being alone with me, and this discussion requires privacy," she said directly. "So I made an appointment."

There was no censure in her tone, but he felt it all the same. "I'm sure that wasn't necessary."

She regarded him coolly but did not argue. She let that lie slide, just as she did so many things. "I wish to speak to you about our...evening appointments."

Alexandre did not care for what that word *did* to him. Elicited physical responses and memories he tried to block out of any time he visited her bedchamber. Which had been far more than he'd anticipated, thinking at *most* it would take a month or two to render her with child.

He blamed the frequency on how difficult it had been to stay away, when he'd known that was the best course of action.

He did not understand the feelings she brought out in him. They didn't make sense. Nothing straightforward. Nothing black-and-white. A messiness. An uncontrollable cyclone of disparate things.

And messiness, a lack of control, these were all purviews of his father. The way his father had felt about his mother. Because no doubt the formidable King Enzo, happy to order people hung for small crimes and other such atrocities, had not known the meaning of love—although he had claimed to love his queen.

A love Alexandre had stolen from him, according to Enzo. A love that had destroyed everything in its wake.

And it was Alexandre's job to fix all his father had destroyed. His mother had told him this with her last breath, so how could it be anything but the most simple and important truth?

Alexandre had to be on constant guard or he could not be the king required of his family and his country. A king who put *them* above all else.

Was this fair to him as a person? Of course not, but it was his role, his task. The *person* could not exist if the crown was meant to lead, protect, save.

So he could not worry himself over Evelyne—he had all the best doctors with her. He could not concern himself with how the appointments with Ines used to make him feel—they were done and over.

"I'm not sure this is something that requires a discussion," Alexandre said stiffly. He did not attend such *appointments* anymore because Alis had its heir in Evelyne's soon-to-be child.

Concern jittered again in his chest, but he shoved it away. He had all the best doctors at her disposal. She would not meet the same fate as their mother had. He simply wouldn't allow it.

Ines held his gaze. Her eyes were the same color blue as the diamonds at her ears and direct. "You have skipped the last three such appointments. You have given me no reason why this is the case. Therefore I would like to discuss it."

She did not say this in any accusatory way *exactly*. But she said it in a way that felt like he had performed some dereliction of duty, and she was the general here to hand out punishment.

He cleared his throat at the strange, uncomfortable uncertainty that settled inside his chest. A king did not have room for uncertainty. Certainly not when it came to his wife.

"I apologize for not being clearer," he said, trying to trot out his regal tone and finding it fell a bit flat with her. Or maybe when discussing *sex* with his wife in the necessary…vague terms. "With an heir now secured, we no longer need to…" He had no other words. Everything became a kind of odd blank.

This was what Ines did to him sometimes. Turned him into a man he did not recognize. Who did not know how to proceed or protect. When everything—*everything*—rested on his ability to do both.

"This is not about an heir to the throne, Alexandre," Ines returned. Her tone remained businesslike, her posture straight and regal. "I wish to be a mother regardless of where our child would fall in the royal hierarchy."

He stared at her for a minute. He got the sense she'd been thinking about this for quite some time. Had practiced these words and this argument, and so it felt somehow like a betrayal. That she would upend his status quo so purposely.

"As the king and queen, it will be our duty to usher Evelyne's child into our world, into being an *heir*. We may not be his parents, but we will have a very important role. Surely this is enough."

She didn't flinch, didn't look down or away. She held herself as still and regal as any queen should. Her gaze was direct, if a little chilly. "It is not enough."

It is not enough. He blinked. Once. Before he remembered himself. Gathered himself. Armored himself. He looked down at her, as he might any recalcitrant employee. Because at the end of the day, his wife *was* a role—not a person. They were titles, not feelings.

He would forgive her for forgetting, but he would not change course.

"Ines, I'm sure you can be reasonable."

"In this I'm afraid I cannot be," she said, sounding the very example of control. "If you are not going to give me a child, then I should like an annulment."

Queen Ines Lidia regarded her husband with as much control as she had left in her. She had begun to think she didn't affect him. That any flashes of temper or passion she had seen over the past year were figments of her own imagination.

But she saw both in his eyes now. Little flickers of a man she knew existed under all the trappings of the title he was so devoted to.

"I understand how divorce is out of the question for you," she continued, keeping her tone reasonable. "But I'm sure your publicity team can work through an annulment." She didn't let herself clutch her hands together like she wanted to. She would *not* look down at her lap. She had to maintain eye contact and certainty. She'd been practicing this conversation for weeks now.

Perhaps she'd had the *tiniest* hope he would simply agree to return to their appointment schedule rather than an annulment, but mostly she had known better. He'd made the decision *not* to come to her bedroom on purpose and with reason.

Alexandre did nothing without his precious reason.

"The timing could not be better," Ines continued, keeping her polite smile in place. "Evelyne having the baby, the *heir*, in the coming days means there will be ample distraction from anything such as an annulment. Any bad press over it shouldn't last long in the face of the new heir being born."

When he didn't speak, she knew he was angrier than he let show on his face.

In some ways, she thought she understood her husband better than anyone. She too knew what it was like to be saddled with a duty far too adult at far too young an age. And she could even admit that Alexandre's duties were far more complex than hers had been. Not just to be a good king, but to be the king that *fixed* everything. It was difficult work. A constant fight. King Enzo had done deep, lasting damage to the country of Alis.

All Ines had been tasked with since she could remember was to bag an important husband so her father's wealth could buy him some influence. She had been trained since birth to be nothing more than some royal's wife.

And she'd succeeded. *Bagged a prince*, as her mother had told her somewhat drunkenly one night before the wedding. Before Enzo had died, her father had enjoyed that royal ear he'd wanted. Of course, Enzo had been chaotic and not very trustworthy, so Ines didn't think it had worked quite the way her father had hoped.

Particularly when Enzo had died and Alexandre had shown no interest in playing her father's games. In those first few months of being a princess, of Alexandre meeting every *appointment*, she'd been happy enough. Then, she'd gotten everything she'd wanted when King Enzo had died, except a child, and her father had gotten *nothing*.

But such satisfactions were short-lived when she was left with no child—and a husband who avoided her.

She would have stayed with Alexandre forever, and maybe even happily, if she had a child. But if he couldn't even bear to visit her bed, she needed something…else.

"You made vows, Ines," he said, enunciating every word like he could turn it into a dagger without any heat or ice behind it. "You knew going in what those vows meant. You cannot simply break them because… we don't see eye to eye."

She made herself breathe carefully before she responded. She'd learned as a child to hide her temper, her reaction. She knew how to keep those things buried deep down, and they would not serve her here anymore than they had served her in her father's house.

But this was more than seeing eye to eye, as he well knew, and his trivializing it was *infuriating*.

"But you are changing the nature of our agreement," Ines argued, keeping her calm even if she had to clasp her hands together to remind herself she had to be centered. "You are changing what that meant. We were meant to have a child. Now you are saying we won't."

There were other things she wanted, but she was giving up on them. Something about seeing Evelyne so happy—with her husband, Gabriel, and with her pregnancy. It was a window into a life Ines had never believed she could have. She had known since birth her only role was to secure her father's status with the royal family. That love would never really matter.

She had done her duty, married the prince, become a queen. She had thought that would be it. And all along she told herself it would be all right because someday she would be a mother, and she would raise a prince or princess to be a good person.

Someday she would have someone to love and love her back.

Perhaps she could have withstood being unhappy forever, Alexandre always at arm's length no matter how she'd come to care for him. There was that care *and* many things she enjoyed about being queen. She got to work with charities, make sure the issues she cared about were supported throughout the country of Alis. She had power and sway and influence, and because of Alexandre's outreach programs, she got to go into the public and *help*. She had not expected to be allowed to be so deeply involved in her people's lives. She had not expected any future royal husband to actually want her input and help.

That had certainly not been her father's way. He'd rather viewed a female child as cattle to be sold off.

So if Evelyne had never returned to the palace—married and pregnant and happy—perhaps Ines would still be going along. Perhaps she would even let Alexandre strip this last dream from her.

But the friendship she'd developed with her sister-in-law had opened her eyes to a different future. Ines liked to think she'd learned a thing or two from Evelyne over the past few months. How to stand up for herself as much as she stood up for others. How to value herself, not bury herself in everyone else's value. Evelyne was not afraid, not dutiful. She stood up to her brother and to her husband.

And life had rewarded her.

So Ines had come to the conclusion that enjoying her duties was not enough. She deserved more.

She would have loved to believe she could get that *more* from Alex. She knew what a good man he was. Underneath all his layers of cold control was a man who desperately wanted to put his country to rights, to undo his father's evil. Ines loved being at his side for that.

But Ines knew she could not get under that control. If he cared about her at all, he saw her as a tool. Not a wife in the true sense of the word. Not even a friend.

So if he would not give her a child, she could not stay.

Her hands shook, so she tightened her grip on them. She did not let herself look away from Alexandre's handsome face, though the grim line of his mouth and the fire of fury danced in his dark eyes.

She had seen him furious before, mostly when his father had been alive, but he always kept it under control. And he did so now.

Perhaps that was why something that was nothing like fear fluttered low in her stomach. Because she didn't *fear* Alexandre. Sometimes she was terribly afraid she was so in love with him that, even if she did leave, she'd never get over it.

Alexandre inhaled deeply, and she braced herself because she knew he would speak once he carefully exhaled.

"Ines, I will not pretend to know what has gotten into you. I suggest you leave at once, and we will simply… forget about this conversation."

Ines squeezed her hands tight enough for her nails to dig into her flesh. She wanted to jump to her feet and *yell*, but she would not. She would *not*. She would be like him. So cool and detached and *certain*.

For once, she would demand what *she* wanted. What *she* deserved.

"I do not want to do that, Alexandre."

"You married into a *system*," he said viciously. "Your wants and desires ceased to matter when you pledged yourself to Alis."

A system. A pawn. Yes, she'd known her role, but in the past year, outside of her father's house and rigid rules and demands, Ines had slowly unfurled. Maybe not outwardly, but inside herself.

Her role no longer felt like some fixed, external cage. It was something *she* got to have some say in. Alexandre could really only blame himself for such a change. He'd let her determine which charities she wanted a role in. He'd given her carte blanche to plan events. He had solicited her opinions on certain matters.

Yes, he was still in charge. Yes, because of years of training she almost always let him have his way, but he'd opened up a new world. He'd given her a small say, and now she understood the phrase *Give them an inch and they'll take a mile*.

Because she wanted so much more than his measly inch.

She stood and let her hands relax at her sides instead

of clench into fists. Because she had stood, and because his manners were so ingrained, he stood as well. He was taller than her, but he'd placed his palms on his desk and leaned forward so they were nearly eye to eye, only the desk between them.

"I pledged myself to Alis, yes," she agreed, keeping her voice quiet enough to feel like she was in control. Because she would not raise her voice to bluster. It didn't work with him. He'd survived too many years of his father. "But I also pledged myself to *you*, Alexandre."

He looked at her like she'd taken to speaking Greek. "This has nothing to do with *me*. Your wish to be a mother is...your own."

She sighed. "It is. But it was part of our agreement, was it not?"

He was stubbornly silent in response.

Ines did not consider herself someone with a temper. She had never been *allowed* temper. Perhaps that's why when it sparked to life now, she let it. "I want a child."

"Well then, by all means. Let us simply get after it right now."

He said it with such savage distaste, she felt the need to meet his disgusted tone with a challenge of her own, to take his snide comment and flip it on its head.

"You know what? Let's. We've the time blocked off, after all." She jerked off her jacket and tossed it aside, watching the muscle in his jaw tic. A strange feeling swept through her. Perhaps it was freedom? She wouldn't know. She'd never had that. And since she hadn't, she chased it.

She began to unbutton her blouse.

"Ines. Enough."

But it wasn't. Not nearly enough. She shrugged out of her shirt, quickly unzipped her skirt and stepped out of it and her shoes. She was in nothing but her underwear. In his *office*. And she felt…

Alive. Ridiculously, foolishly alive. In charge. In control. Not once in twenty-five years on this planet had she ever felt this. Maybe a *fraction* of it a few months back when she'd insisted that Alexandre *must* interfere with Gabriel's thick-skulled abandonment of Evelyne.

But this…this was a freedom she'd never felt. She was a *storm*. Powerful. About to do *damage*.

So she did not cower, as she might once have done. She did not wilt at his icy, disapproving stare. At the way he could look like an imposing mountain, all broad shoulders and dark hair and eyes. So much larger than her. So much more powerful.

Except, whatever flickered in his gaze made *her* feel like the powerful one.

She crossed the distance between them, pressed her body to his. He held himself stiffly, even as his heat wrapped around her.

And he did not push her away, when he had all the physical power to do so. His nostrils flared, his gaze was angry, but he did not set her apart from him.

So she hooked her arm up around his neck and pulled his mouth down to hers.

And then she kissed him with all this newfound wildness, as she'd never once kissed him before.

She expected cold dismissal. Perhaps even a kind of pleasant response before carefully setting her back and telling her *no*. She expected so many things.

Except that he shudder out a breath when she pulled his bottom lip between her teeth.

Except that his hand clamped on her hip, strong and steadying.

Certainly not his other hand moving up her spine, the strong, hot weight of his palm a drug in and of itself. Then his fingers were in her hair, tensing into a fist. The pressure a delightful frisson of pleasure that twisted into violent want and need when he pulled enough to get her mouth away from his.

The slight prick of pain in her scalp fused with a dark pleasure of his kiss, his body, so that her knees grew weak, her body *pulsed*. She thought it would take nothing at all for an orgasm to sweep through her.

She had enjoyed sex each and every time they'd engaged in it, but *this*? This was something else entirely. The word *enjoy* had no place here. It was too tame. Too small.

He held her back from his mouth, his eyes dark and wild, his breathing as ragged as hers, his hands still a fist in her hair. She watched him try to fight for some control, some sense of the usual *Alexandre*.

But he couldn't find it.

CHAPTER TWO

It was insanity. The pulsing, sexual haze that surrounded him was utter insanity. It was a spell, and he had to be strong enough to break it.

She had tested his control and resolve before, but only in the bedroom, only in his own mind. Never with demands. Never with wants of her own.

Nothing like this.

He held her there, a terrifying thrill of power flowing through him. She was in his grip. She was *his* to do what he wished with. She was such a tiny little thing in stature, but the curves she carefully downplayed in her royal outfits were on plain display in nothing but her underwear.

Ivory skin. Soft. Warmth. *Life*. Her cheeks were flushed, her breath as ragged as his. Her blue eyes wide, but there was nothing like *fear* or *concern* in that gaze. No, it was all want.

Underscored by the fact her hands were carefully undoing the buttons of his perfectly pressed shirt, all the while she looked right back at him.

She was just so warm. She smelled as she always did, some alluring mix of citrus and vanilla. It existed in her skin, deep in her hair, everywhere. Now it wound around him like some opiate haze.

Her hands pushed the shirt open so that his chest and stomach were bared to her. She leaned forward, and his hand in her hair allowed the forward movement. As she pressed an open mouth kiss just over his heart.

Then lower. She undid his belt, the button of his pants, his zipper, and he watched her as if outside himself. She tilted her head up, and he still did not let go of her hair, but he let her continue to move down his body.

She held his gaze the entire time she sank to her knees, even as she wrapped her hand around the base of him, guided the hard, throbbing length of him into her mouth.

He hissed out a breath.

They had never done this. They could not be doing this. *This* did not beget children, which was the only reason he'd ever been with her in the first place. Heirs. Duty. To be sure, it had always ended up being pleasurable, but not solely for the sake of pleasure.

This was.

Her mouth hot and sweet. Her eyes that vibrant blue that held him in some kind of vise. Her hands on his still-clothed thighs as she took him as deep as her inexperience allowed.

He would come undone in mere seconds if he let her continue such a thing. He would stop this. Here. Now. A lapse in sanity. A momentary weakness.

When King Alexandre was *strong*.

He pulled her away from him by her hair, the sound

she made—a keening kind of moan—arrowing through him, tearing all his determination to ribbons.

He released her hair and pulled her up from her knees and in one swift move deposited her on his desk. He kissed her, deep and rough, wildfire in his veins. Pounding through him so hard he couldn't hear any more of his thoughts.

He unsnapped the enclosure of her bra and filled his palms with the perfect weight of her breasts. They moaned together this time. The warmth of her skin, so human, so real, so soft. His. *His*.

The desk was at the perfect height to spread her legs wide, to step in between them, to slowly, torturously rub against where she was wild and ready. Her desire ripe around them as he kissed her deeper and deeper.

There was some distant alarm in his head. His office. His desk. His *control* tattered on the ground, but he could still pick it up, salvage this mess.

"Alex," she panted into his mouth. She almost never called him Alex. Not even in the throes of passion. Usually only when she was angry with him.

Now she panted it. Angry? Maybe. But not *only* angry. His name was as much demand as it was *plea*.

He thought himself a better man, and it only took his arranged bride to undo all of that.

And then he was inside her, and she *moaned*, erupting around him in great, clenching waves. Wanton and careless. He'd known he could push her here, and yet he always held himself back.

Wild was the enemy.

But it had won today, because he moved inside her

chasing all that wildness. All that desperation. She moved against him, held on to him, chanted his name in pleading, pleasured glory. She touched him, and somehow she made him feel like a person—hot-blooded and real—instead of what he had to be: an icon. A statue. An immovable force of good.

She kissed him—her mouth was soft, reverent. Like she might care for him beyond all he had to be.

He had no space for that, even as it wound inside of him like a drug. Even as he stopped holding back from his own crashing orgasm.

The moment was intense. It made him feel like someone else. Like a man. Any man. Not a king. Not the man tasked with undoing his father's horrid mistakes.

Just a man. The weight of it enough to make him unsteady.

And even in his brain-melted state, he knew unsteady was the enemy.

He removed himself from her, blinking back into reality even as his body still pumped in sluggish pleasure.

His office. His *day*. He did not have time for *this*. He'd be late. For all the tower of things that must be done.

God knew he hadn't even locked the *door*. What if someone had come in and seen him in such an animalistic state? It would have been a disaster in a million different ways.

And she dared to sit on his desk, naked and mussed from *him*, looking...sated. *Smiling*. It stoked a fury in him that he knew was the tainted blood of his father. But he would not ever cross a line into violence, into fury.

That did not mean he had it in him to be *kind*. "I hope you're happy."

* * *

Ines *was* happy. Oh, it wouldn't last, considering he was about to ruin it all, but that had been…

Glorious. Wondrous. Altering.

Except it hadn't altered him. Well, for a moment it had, but now they were back to stone cold King Alexandre. Maybe with a little more panic, but he was reining it in, even as she sat on his desk—*naked*—still trying to catch her breath.

But now, in a stark kind of clarity, she understood why she'd believed he could never return her feelings for him. He always saw to her pleasure during their *appointments*, and she knew he found some of his own. But it was always…a kind of detachment. He never caused her pain, was always gentle and attentive, and obviously came to his own…conclusion. Or there would be no expectation of a baby, after all.

But never this wild, fiery thing. Never this loss of control. Never seeing who he was underneath all those brick walls he built for himself.

But now?

She reached out to touch him, and he sidestepped away from her hand. He bent over, picked up her discarded clothes and handed them to her.

She didn't take them at first.

"We didn't even lock the door, Ines."

He sounded so disgusted. She thought she should feel some kind of shame as he did, but she could not find any inside of her. Perhaps when the aftershocks of it all wore off, but she rather thought it was hardly the end of the world to get caught up with one's *spouse*.

She took the clothes. "I do not know that anyone would be all that shocked that a man and his wife might share a morning *appointment*." She slid off the desk and began to pull her clothes back on—because the door *was* still unlocked.

"Perhaps they would not be shocked, but people have *phones*, Ines. Would you be quite so casual if pictures of your naked body were sold to tabloids around the world?"

Ines blinked, his words like a bucket of cold water. She shivered against them. "Perhaps not," she managed to say. "But it seems you are reaching for the worst-possible scenario."

"Yes, that is my *job*. My duty."

She sighed. She knew he felt that way, but she did not know how he lived under the weight of that. She kept trying to save him from the weight of that, but he never listened to her. Never considered her. Not when it came to *them* as people. "It does not always have to be about duty. Not *always*." She stepped forward, wanting to reach out and touch him, knowing he would only avoid it again. "Sometimes it could be about *us*, if you'd let it."

He made a dismissive sort of noise. "I am going to be late for my meeting with the French diplomat. A meeting I cannot afford to be late for. You must leave at once."

He did not look at her. A million feelings crashed around in her chest. She even gave half a thought to causing another scene. Be the storm. Be in charge.

But for the moment she was a bit too bruised. She

wanted to retreat, and wasn't this whole thing about getting what she wanted?

So she followed the impulse. She left his office saying nothing else. She tidied herself up and met with all her appointments that day, but neither her heart nor her head were truly in it.

They were both back in his office, reliving that moment over and over in her head.

She wanted it to mean something. She wanted it to mean *everything*. She even fantasized about it.

If she pressed for the annulment, would there be a repeat performance?

Or would he relent and give her what she didn't want but thought she probably needed?

She was too terrified of the second option, but she did not know how to continue like this. She wanted to be a *person*, not *only* a queen. A *human being*, not only a statue.

He wanted the opposite. Whether he *should* or not did not matter, because it was what he wanted.

Almost a year of being his dutiful wife had not changed anything for him. Her *goodness* had not suddenly made him any different. Even that unexpected loss of control and blazing passion had not changed anything for him.

She had realized sometime in the past few weeks it never would, and today only confirmed that. So how should she proceed? How could she save herself from the relentless weight of wanting to be a mother? Wanting him to love her—knowing he never would?

If he would not give her the annulment, what then?

A knock sounded at her bedroom door where she sat at the mirror getting ready for dinner. Before she could respond, it opened, and Alexandre stood there. He did not cross the threshold.

"Evelyne has had the baby."

For a moment, the words couldn't arrange themselves in a way that made sense. His sister. Baby. *The baby.*

Her nephew had been born. Ines knew she should feel elation, but for a moment there was only a sharp stab of pain at the idea that she could not seem to find love and a future for herself. "Oh."

"She would like us to come meet him."

Ines gathered herself. There were some things that no matter how she was feeling, no matter how much she wanted to *change* them, she still had to put on a queen's mask and face. This was one of those things.

Not because it was *business*, but because regardless of what went on between her and Alexandre, her nephew had been born.

Will he be my nephew if Alexandre allows an annulment?

That thought ached. But she shook it away because no matter what Evelyne was her *friend*. They would remain friends.

She rose. "Yes, of course."

She crossed the room, but Alex did not move. He stood in her doorway, a disapproving, concrete mountain.

But he hadn't been that in his office this morning. Certainly not when she'd lowered herself to her knees and—

"Before we go down to her room, I would like you to know I've given your request the necessary consideration." He stood there, stiff and formal, hands clasped behind his back. He *appeared* to be looking at her, but he was not *truly* meeting her gaze.

She studied his dark eyes, fascinated by this slight change. This slight sign of…cowardice.

"An annulment is unlikely, though not fully out of the question. This delicate situation will require time and thought and careful planning," he said, his voice toneless. "I do not wish to use my nephew's birth as a distraction for anything so…distasteful. Since it will take some time, and you no doubt do not wish to remain in the palace, I will arrange somewhere for you to live. Out of the way. Private."

Her mouth dropped open. She had not expected him to simply sign off on an annulment. She had definitely expected refusal. But this was…

"You're…sending me away?"

"Not immediately. You will stay put until we know…" He glanced down at her stomach. As he so often had in the past year. They never said words like *not pregnant* or *no baby*. It was all code words and glances at the parts of her body that seemed honor-bound to betray her while offering no medical answers for *why*.

Stay put. He wanted her to stay put. But if she was *not* pregnant in a few weeks, as would no doubt be the case considering the past eleven months, he would send her into *exile*. While he and he alone worked out the *details*.

She forced herself to breathe normally as she began to see spots. Perhaps it was rage. Perhaps it was a rage *stroke*. She wasn't quite certain. But he turned on a heel and walked away.

To see Evelyne. To meet the baby.

And she would *stay put*, while he adjusted everything to suit himself.

No. No, she couldn't allow that. The certainty of that was like a tsunami of purpose, but an argument would be pointless. He was the king.

So she said nothing. She followed him to Evelyne and Gabriel's wing and tried very hard to force a believable smile for the pair as they entered the bedroom.

Evelyne was in bed, a bundle in her arms. Gabriel's hip rested on the edge of the bed, looking down at both his wife and the baby.

Ines did not look at Alex. She stayed on one side of the bed, while he went to the other.

Ines looked at the baby. Just the tiniest thing. His eyes closed, his round face relaxed and content. It brought a wave of love and envy. Joy and pain. She blinked back some tears, looked up at Evelyne.

Luckily her sister-in-law's eyes were on her son, so she would not see the tears in Ines's own eyes. She just looked exhaustedly at peace.

Ines *felt* the love and joy she so wanted to experience. She felt a wave of love for this little bundle who was her nephew.

Or not, depending on how Alexandre *worked things out*. Details *he* got to choose. Instead of doing the *sane* thing and agreeing to return to their *appointment* schedule, he was going to send her away.

No. No, he didn't get to do that. He didn't get to decide. If anything made it clear it was this new *life*—a life that brought Evelyne and Gabriel so much joy in the moment. She wanted that.

If Alexandre wouldn't give that to her, she would not be his pawn, his tool, his *anything*. She would not be *sent away*. She would not live her life at *his* whim.

She was the storm.

For the first time in her life, *she* was going to decide.

CHAPTER THREE

It took nearly forty-eight hours to realize Ines was missing. Alexandre had been avoiding her, and he'd been so wrapped up in diplomatic meetings that also required meetings with his bloodthirsty general he was still trying to get rid of without starting a bloody *coup* that he had simply assumed she was avoiding him as much as he was avoiding her.

He had heard no rumblings about missed appointments. He had heard nothing of her not being where she was *meant to be*. And since *he* had avoided meals with her, no one had bothered to inform him that *she* had not been taking meals at *all*.

Apparently because she had planned it quite carefully. Her assistant—also missing—had quietly and carefully rearranged all of Ines's appointments—canceling, rescheduling, taking care of them via *email*.

Then there was the fact no one even knew what car she'd taken or even what day Ines had *actually* left the palace. Since he had gutted his father's insane border patrol with checkpoints everywhere, leaving only what was necessary, it would be easy enough to slip out of the country unnoticed.

And so she likely had.

But it *would* require planning, and the conclusion Alexandre had come to was that it had also required *help*—from more than just her loyal assistant. There was no way disappearing for *days* without being found out could have happened without the most *personal* intel.

So he went in search of his sister, doing his level best to maintain the roiling anger underneath an outer wall of frigid calm. He'd had such practice at hiding his feelings, it was second nature.

Why didn't it feel like second nature today? Why did it feel like he'd been split open and his insides were pouring out of him? Why did the anger feel akin to grief? Why was everything so damn confusing?

Ines.

Perhaps she was the punishment his father had wanted for him after all.

When he found his sister, Evelyne was sitting alone in one of the parlors. She was sipping tea with her eyes closed. She looked tired. In any other situation, he might have reconsidered making demands of her.

But his wife had *run away*, and someone had *helped her do it*. Evelyne had survived labor, and though he worried about her sitting here alone in silence, the doctors had assured him everything had gone exactly as it should, and Evelyne was as healthy as could be.

And his wife *was missing*. He gritted his teeth together and stepped into the room.

Evelyne's eyes blinked open. "Oh, hello, Alexandre." She closed her eyes again. "I'm a bit busy right now."

He looked at her dubiously. She was curled up on the settee, drinking tea, no baby to be seen. Eyes *closed*.

She opened them again, narrowed them. *"Shoo."*

He stared at his sister for a full minute. "I beg your pardon?"

She sighed heavily. "Sorry." She did not sound the least bit apologetic. "I have thirty minutes of alone time to sit with my tea in silence while Gabriel takes care of Gabriel." Her irritable scowl softened into a smile. "I suppose there are some downsides to naming your child after his father. It gets rather confusing, but we can't decide on a nickname. *I* think Gabby is quite nice. Gabriel thinks Gabri. They're near the same, are they not? So why not just go with mine? *I'm* the one who had to push him out of my body, aren't I?" She waved a regal hand in dismissal. *"Anyway*, this is my quiet alone time. You're not invited."

He let his sister prattle on, but he did not pretend to care about what she was saying. "Where is she?"

Evelyne's eyebrows drew together. "Who?"

"Ines," he ground out.

"How should I know?" She gave a careless shrug, then after a moment seemed to take on at least some of the gravity of the situation. She studied him, tilting her head slightly. "You've lost your wife, Alexandre?" she tsked and shook her head. "What a shame, though I can hardly blame her the way you stomp about."

He did not trust his voice right away. He breathed through the fury and some other feeling he did not know how to label.

Evelyne must have recognized *some* note of seriousness in his expression, because she sobered. "Alex, I haven't seen Ines. I've been exhausted and out of sorts, what with having a *baby three days ago.* And... Well, to be honest, I thought perhaps she was feeling a little tender over the baby, and that's why I haven't seen her. So I haven't asked after her. Perhaps she's in the library."

"She has been missing from the palace for nearly three days."

Evelyne blinked, looking well and truly shocked. But his sister *was* a good actress. "She ran away?"

"You're telling me you had nothing to do with this?"

Evelyne's gaze got a little cool. She leveled him with a hard look, but there was a softness in her eyes. "I would help Ines in a lot of ways and support her in more, but I wouldn't do either at the cost of you."

It hurt, because he knew she was telling him the truth, and he did not fully deserve the high opinion she had of him. Yes, he'd tried to protect her, and yes, he had tasked Gabriel with saving her from having to marry the awful General Vinyes last year, but there were also so many ways he'd failed her since she'd been a baby.

And still she saw him as a hero, even when he wasn't one in the least. Father had still hurt her—physically, emotionally. No matter what stumbling blocks Alexandre had managed to erect, he had not been fully capable of protecting Evelyne.

"What will you do?" Evelyne asked gently. In the here and now. Married to a man she loved. Mother to a child she would love—better than anyone. It was not his doing that she had managed to find a good life. At best, he'd helped her survive. *She* was the one who'd figured out how to thrive.

While his wife had *run away* from him. Like *he* was a monster. Like *he'd* done something wrong, when all he'd done was work hard to do what was right, needed.

What would he do?

His reply was not gentle. "Find her."

The days stretched out long, uncomfortable and nerve-racking. Ines had never rebelled before in *any* way—not against her father, not against Alexandre—her two captors, more or less.

Well, she supposed asking Alexandre for an annulment was *kind of* a rebellion. An easing into it. Asking permission to be allowed to rebel? It hadn't felt so much scary as exhilarating, necessary, groping for *change*.

The way he'd reacted hadn't exactly *scared* her. It had given her hope. That maybe here in the life she hadn't chosen was something she *could* choose.

Him.

Then disappointment. Because he'd never choose her.

But now, running away, she felt like she'd taken a dive into an icy ocean. She was cold and scared and lost at sea.

If not for Jonet, she would have turned back. To the comfortable and familiar, even if it was a little miserable.

Jonet was Ines's cousin and oldest friend, who Alexandre had allowed Ines to hire as her personal assistant. Jonet's loyalty was not to Alis or Alexandre, but to Ines. So when Ines had asked her to make the runaway arrangements, Jonet had jumped to do just that.

Jonet was handling all the travel. Keeping Ines out of

sight as much as possible and doing all she could to keep her moves from being easily found out by Alexandre.

He was a king with endless resources, so no doubt he *would* find her. She was not so foolish to think this was permanent, but if she could make it *hard* on him…

Well, maybe it was childish to want to punish him. Maybe she was childish. Maybe the *new* Ines could be childish and brave and terrified—all at the same time.

After a few days of crisscrossing Europe, keeping a low profile while Jonet handled things, they were now walking up a quaint, dirt walk to a small cottage in the middle of a forest. Ines did not know what country they were in, and she would not ask.

She did know they were meant to stay here for a while, as Jonet was satisfied they had not been followed.

Jonet marched forward, shoved a key into the lock and opened the door. She stepped inside, and Ines followed.

Inside it was dim, and all the furniture was covered. It was a bit musty, but nothing alarming.

"Home sweet home," Jonet said brightly.

It reminded Ines a bit of a fairy tale. Like Princess Aurora's cottage, and Jonet was her little fairy godmother flitting about making everything okay and safe. It left Ines feeling a strange kind of exhausted. She simply wanted to find a bed to sleep in for perhaps as long as Aurora had slept after pricking her finger.

"Jonet, I will never be able to repay you."

"Let us not worry about repayments just yet." Jonet moved into what Ines realized was the kitchen area. "It's a bit rustic," she said. "I know you're not used to that, but luckily for you, I am." While Ines's father had always had money and they'd always lived in luxury, Jonet's mother had married a man considered *beneath the family's* means. She had not grown up poor exactly, but there had certainly been lean times for Jonet's family—and Ines's father had refused to help his sister monetarily.

That was the kind of man her father was. Selfish. A little mean. But Ines had always lived comfortably. She knew her guilt over what Jonet had dealt with as a child was unwarranted, and certainly unwelcome, but she felt it all the same.

Jonet fiddled with the stove and started a fire in it, while Ines stood in the middle of the small cottage feeling more at a loss than she ever had in her whole life. Was running away any better than staying? Was having Jonet handle everything really the mark of a brave woman taking charge of her own life, her own wants?

Jonet looked over her shoulder at Ines. "Why don't you pull off all the furniture coverings? We'll get settled in."

Right. Something to do. She wasn't a queen here. She was a person like any other. She was *herself*, just like she'd always wanted to be. She tried to move toward the living room to remove the furniture coverings, but her legs wouldn't move.

Ines couldn't fathom why, but the only thing she could seem to do was stand there and sob as though she'd just lost *everything*.

CHAPTER FOUR

ALEXANDRE WAS NOT his father. He reminded himself of this as he made plans to find his runaway wife.

He would not track her down like prey. He would be civilized.

They would be civilized, even if her running away was decidedly *not*. Even if every time he thought about her *sneaking out of the palace* with that *cousin* of hers, something hot and mean erupted inside him.

But he would control it. All of it. He summoned Gabriel to his office so that it was clear it was *official* business. So that he could have a reminder that he was a good, calm, controlled king here in his minimalist office—the opposite of his father's gaudy, gilt one that Alexandre had gutted and turned into a soft, feminine office for Ines.

History be damned. His father be damned.

Gabriel came into the office, settled himself on a chair casually. "Evelyne told me Ines has...disappeared."

"Yes, I'd like to hire your company to find her, but this cannot be official business—for the palace or for you." Perhaps it *was* royal business to track down the country's queen, but Alexandre didn't love the optics of that.

Gabriel ran a security company for many royals and wealthy people. He had contacts all over the world. And maybe finding a runaway wife wasn't *security*, but it was something Gabriel's outfit could no doubt handle, especially now that he wasn't just Gabriel Marti, but *Lord* Gabriel Marti, the title he'd been given upon marrying Evelyne.

"Luckily my company specializes in off-the-books," Gabriel replied.

"Yes. Well." *Off-the-books* left him feeling a bit... *oily*. It was not how he operated, but...sometimes a king had to go against the grain. As long as it was for good, for the right reasons, it had to be okay. As long as it was handled *appropriately*, and not at all like his father.

"I'll need to ask you a few questions before I can decide how to proceed," Gabriel said, watching Alexandre carefully.

And since they had been friends since they were boys, Alexandre knew Gabriel saw too much. Still, he ignored what was in his friend's expression. Concern. Perhaps, worse, understanding.

"Why would Ines run away?" Gabriel asked, his voice very neutral. None of Evelyne's commentary on his *stomping about*, as she called it.

"I have no idea."

"Alexandre." Gabriel sighed, leaning his elbows onto his knees. "I do not know your wife nearly as well as I know you, but she has never once struck me as someone to just...fly off the handle. Even if she was, there would still be an inciting incident." His gaze was direct. "It would help if I knew it. It's easier to find where someone has run away to, if one knows *what* they're running *from*."

Alex supposed it was his friend's directness, and lack of blame, and the fact that they understood each other as few others did that allowed him to relent a *little*.

"There was…nothing. A small disagreement, I suppose, about what our future was to look like. But there were no…dramatics." Unless wild sex on this very desk counted. But much as he might like to convince himself *that* was what had sent her packing, he knew it had been his reaction to it.

Much as he'd like to pretend it was the opposite.

"I…" Gabriel shifted in his seat, a sure sign of discomfort that Alexandre found *very* off-putting. "I did hear you and Ines arguing the day Gabri was born."

Alexandre could only blink. He had argued with Ines briefly before it had turned into…well, something he hadn't quite been able to put out of his mind, particularly with how often he was required to sit at this very desk.

He shook his head. "The matter was settled. She made no threats. There was no discussion of leaving." Just him sending her away…

"Perhaps *you* thought the matter was settled, but this points to…well, her feeling otherwise. Don't you think?"

Alexandre shook his head because it did not make *sense*. "I simply could not give her what she wanted. She understood this. She said—" No, she had never come out and said she understood. He had taken her usual quiet distance as her customary agreement.

"So you disagreed on…personal, marriage matters? For your future?"

"Yes, I..." Alexandre cleared his throat. If there was anyone he could be honest with, it was Gabriel. Gabriel knew that the marriage had been arranged by his father for the most part. And if explaining the truth would help find Ines, help fix this whole situation, there was really no harm in Gabriel knowing.

Besides, Ines running away because of *this* was... She was in the wrong. "I did not think we needed to pursue having a child since the heir has been taken care of. She...disagreed."

Gabriel did not say anything to that. For a moment, his study was done in utter silence, and Alexandre could not see through it. Could not read his friend's expression. Something he had always been able to do...

At least, before Gabriel had fallen in love with Evelyne and married her. Something about that seemed to open up another dimension of Gabriel that Alexandre could not fully comprehend.

Didn't want to.

"Perhaps she simply needed a break from the palace and its fishbowl quality after such a disagreement," Gabriel said. "It's quite possible she will return all on her own after a nice holiday. Still, I will handle tracking her down, quietly and carefully."

"I..." Alexandre was at war with himself. What did he want out of this? He *wanted* to drag her back to the palace, lecture her for such a dereliction of duty, demand... something. Something.

But all of these reactions felt like ones too close to King Enzo. And still, he could hardly let his country know his wife had found fault with him and run away.

Queen Ines was *beloved*. Alexandre had not yet been hailed the hero to his people that he'd hoped to be.

Because he would *not* be his father. "I want to be assured she is okay and safe. I do not wish to…" He did not know how to find the words, but Gabriel stood. He put his hand on Alexandre's shoulder.

"Understood."

And Gabriel had to understand. He had also lived in fear of King Enzo as a boy. He had helped Alexandre save Evelyne from one of his father's plots.

So Alexandre sat back and let Gabriel handle this. He did not ask for updates. He did not demand *action*, though days dragged on with none of those things.

It took nearly a month—between Gabriel carefully choosing the right man to track Ines down to making sure the investigation was quiet, careful and involved no threats.

Finally, Ines had emailed Evelyne at one point to assure her she was fine, and it was the break Gabriel's man needed.

They'd traced her to a small Italian village, living out of town a ways in a *cabin* with her traitorous cousin.

"I can have someone bring her home," Gabriel said, his voice devoid of any emotion, but Alexandre knew there would be judgment based on how he responded.

Alexandre shook his head. "No."

"Evelyne and I could handle things here for a day or two if you'd like to collect her yourself."

"Not yet."

Gabriel's eyebrows rose. "You want her to…stay there?"

He did not. He wanted to drag her home, lecture her, demand to know what the hell she had been thinking.

He wanted his *mouth* on her—and this was the main thing that made his decision for him.

All of these overly emotional responses were not acceptable. So perhaps it would be best if she just…stayed where she was. This was, essentially, his plan. Get her away so he could *think*.

So let her hide. Let her think she'd done some great runaway. What did it hurt? It got him exactly what he'd been planning on anyway—though *he* would have done it with more tact and a PR plan in place. Still, it wasn't so different.

That idea *almost* got through the red haze of anger.

"Yes, for the time being. Let her have her runaway. As long as I know where she is, what she is up to, that is enough for the time being." He could rest. Relax. And be safe from losing his hold on everything with her an entire country away.

While he got everything sorted—determined if an annulment was even *possible*, this was better.

"All right." It was not approval. If anything, there was a tinge of disapproval in his tone.

But Alexandre knew this was the right way to handle it, whether Gabriel approved or not. Ines would be too far away to tempt him, to needle him. But he would know she was safe and he wouldn't worry that she would chafe under his demands. She would think *she* was in control.

Let her.

"I need someone to watch her though. Completely hands-off. Just keeping tabs."

"I'll make sure of it."

"Thank you."

But Gabriel didn't leave. He hesitated, which wasn't like him at all. So Alex braced himself for whatever Gabriel would say.

"Eventually your country is going to want to know why they haven't seen their queen for so long," he said softly, gently even.

"Yes," Alexandre agreed.

But today was not *eventually*.

Nor would tomorrow be.

Ines was miserable in so many different ways she couldn't even catalog them all. She'd stopped worrying about Alexandre finding her. Maybe it was foolish to let her guard down, but she couldn't seem to muster the mental energy.

She was tired. Achy. Nauseous. A flu that came and went, ebbed and flowed, but never disappeared. At least, she kept telling herself it was the flu. Even though she began to suspect something else.

She couldn't let herself engage in that possibility, though. It was too hopeful a thought. Too *awful* a thought. All mixed together into one big fat mess.

Impossible messes were not new to her. She'd been in what had felt like a few in her life. Being promised in marriage to a man she didn't know, a prince she had no concept of, had been her duty. That had felt like a potential sticky mess at the time.

Then she'd been introduced to Alexandre. He'd been so handsome and kind. Not as aloof as he could be now.

No, in the beginning he had been almost *warm*. He had at least always tried to put her at ease, tried to engage in *some* charm.

Now that she'd been around him—and his father—she understood what Alexandre had been doing. Maybe his father had picked her out, thanks to her father's fortune, but Alexandre did not wish to make *her* a victim of King Enzo.

Alexandre was not like King Enzo. Sometimes she wondered if she only loved Alex because he was the bright spot of good in King Enzo's kingdom. But she'd watched Alexandre both under King Enzo's rule and since the old bastard had died.

Alex was a man who put others' needs before his own. He was a man who endeavored to be all the good his father had not been. He could be cold. He certainly kept his *real* self hidden behind a mask.

But sometimes, very rarely, she'd seen underneath the mask—not when he was being kind or even sweet—like in the early days before the wedding when they'd take walks in the garden and he'd made some attempt to get to know her—what she liked and didn't, her hobbies, her interests. The true Alex didn't show up in all that planned *warmth*.

No, the true Alexandre came out in darker moments. When he'd sent his sister away to save her but worried over her. When Evelyne had returned married to Gabriel and very pregnant and Alexandre had been conflicted about his best friend's role. After his father's death when he'd felt guilt over not feeling grief—and he'd let her comfort him.

In his office, when anger had finally snapped some band of control, and he hadn't held anything back.

Her heart ached thinking about him, considering that the one moment he'd lost control might have created… She shook her head, refusing to engage with the thought.

She would soon find she wasn't pregnant at all. It was just the stress. Or perhaps these physical issues were simply about not acclimating to the water at the cabin or some such.

If you think that's the case, why won't you see a doctor? Jonet had demanded that a few days ago when Ines had once again been miserable.

Ines had not had much of a response to that. She'd made noises about being afraid Alexandre would find her if she sought medical attention, but it wasn't true.

If he hadn't found her by now…he wasn't trying to find her. Perhaps he hadn't even noticed she was gone. Didn't care. Perhaps he'd told the whole kingdom she'd simply disappeared, and they were all better off.

None of that really made any sense, but she didn't have the energy to figure out what *did* make sense. She just sank into the certainty he didn't want her.

And that was fine, because she didn't want *him*. Not…not the way they'd been doing things. A wall always in between them, except when something terrible happened or when he deigned to visit her bed.

On the verge of tears again, Ines looked up as the front door swung open. Jonet marched into the cottage, carrying bags from the market, interrupting Ines's pity party. *Thank goodness.*

"I've brought you something from the market," Jonet

announced loftily. Something about her hard expression had Ines's stomach fluttering in concern.

"I hope it's more ginger ale," Ines offered with a pleasant smile. It did nothing to change Jonet's expression.

"There is that. Also this." Jonet pulled a box from one of her bags and walked it over to where Ines lay on the couch.

Ines took the proffered box and tried to read the label. Her Italian was patchy at best, but she read English quite well, and underneath the larger print of Italian, in smaller print in English it read *early pregnancy test*.

She looked up at her cousin. How had Jonet come to the conclusion Ines was so desperately trying to avoid?

"You need to know," Jonet said firmly. "You cannot keep wallowing. We need answers so we can decide what to do. Go on then."

Ines opened her mouth to argue, but Jonet was clearly determined. "If you are not pregnant, you will need to see a doctor to see what is wrong with you. If you are, you will also need to see a doctor to make sure you and a potential baby are healthy. So this is the only step to take." She pulled Ines to her feet and then into the bathroom. "Do not come out until the test is done."

Then she left and closed the door smartly behind her.

Ines blew out a shaky breath. She looked at the offensive box. She could…lie. To Jonet. To herself.

And where would that get you?

Well, wallowing. Which she had to admit, she'd been… *enjoying* wasn't the right word. But it felt nice after years of denying herself every emotional reaction to swamp herself in this one. She was not required to think or act or know. She could just feel.

But now she needed to know. As much as she'd rather continue the wallow, Jonet pointing out she'd need a doctor either way was... Well, it was one thing to deny concerns about her own health, another to deny what might be going on if...if...

She looked at the box. Why was she avoiding this so much?

Because you know.

And the test confirmed all her suspicions.

After a year of desperately trying and having *no* luck, they'd engaged in reckless, angry sex in his office and conceived a child.

She leaned against the sink, eyes closed, emotion swamping her. How could this *be*? Why couldn't it have happened months ago? Everything would be different. *Everything.*

Jonet tapped on the door and then opened it. She stepped in, looked at the test on the sink, then nodded.

"Would you like to call Alexandre?" Jonet asked gently.

"God no." Ines couldn't imagine explaining this to him over the phone. Or at all. Not in this moment, anyway.

"Return to the palace?"

Ines shook her head. Go back there? With this news? After he'd... He didn't want a child. He didn't want *this*.

"Then what, Ines?"

"I don't know." A baby. Finally. This thing she'd wanted for so long, and now it was here at the worst possible time. She slid a hand over her flat stomach. She was elation and joy and dread and disappointment, all in one body.

She swallowed at the wave of nausea. Proof there was a *baby*. A baby *she* wanted, even if he didn't. The thing she'd left him over. How could she listen to any of the negative thoughts when this was everything she wanted?

"I will need a doctor," she said, finding some strength in the idea of a baby, a child. Hers. *Hers*. Yes, Alexandre's too, but he'd rejected this possibility. Which meant it was *hers*. Hers to decide. Hers to protect. Hers to consider *everything* for.

"Yes," Jonet agreed.

"There's no point in letting Alexandre in on this until I know for sure," she said. "Until I have a medical opinion. Until…"

"Until you decide what *you* want."

Ines blinked at Jonet. Yes…yes. What *she* wanted. For herself. For her baby. She would have to tell him, but she got to decide how and when. It didn't have to be right away. She had a right to determine how *she* wanted to handle this before she involved someone who'd made it clear they didn't want this.

Ines nodded. "Yes, I'll tell him once I have figured everything out. For right now, though, we'll just…stay put. Okay?"

Ines ignored the questions and indecision on Jonet's face and took her cousin's *Okay* at face value.

CHAPTER FIVE

THE FIRST TIME Gabriel informed Alexandre that a man had visited Ines and Jonet's cabin—and said man was a doctor—Alexandre had felt a panic unlike anything he'd ever felt before.

He thought of his mother. Of blood. Screams. The doctor at a loss while everything crashed and died around him.

He had not given in to the panic, the memories though. If he gave in to panic now, everything in his kingdom would unravel. And, since no one was taken from the cabin in some kind of emergency vehicle, no bodies emerged, Alexandre knew that whatever was *wrong* was…fine.

The second time, a month later, he might have flown off the handle if Gabriel hadn't pointed out it was exactly a month from the first appointment—down to the date and time, so likely some kind of follow-up. Nothing new to be concerned about. Not an emergency of any kind.

The third time… Well, he might have stormed over to Italy that very second if Evelyne had not delivered a calm, direct question.

"Is there any way she could be pregnant?"

He had stared at her sister, sitting on the floor with baby Gabri, who seemed to grow at an exponential rate, all the while remaining impossibly small.

Sometimes Evelyne handed him to Alexandre, and Alex felt like he was five years old again, holding baby Evelyne because Father refused to let the nursemaids *coddle* her.

He didn't care for the reminder of such a helpless feeling—knowing he needed to be strong for Evelyne, for his lost mother. And not having a clue as to *how*.

But this question, this *possibility* that Ines might...

Evelyne looked up, seemed to note the shock on Alexandre's face and explained herself.

"She told me there was nothing medical in the way, according to your doctors. So unless you...hadn't been together." Evelyne pulled a face as she gazed down at the baby in her lap. "A monthly doctor's appointment *could* point to a baby. Perhaps more likely than some monthly illness if the doctor's visits are happening exactly a month apart."

Alexandre supposed he heard the words, absorbed them, but they left him in a strange in-between world. He did not know how to move forward from this simple question.

Is there any way she could be pregnant?

There was precisely *one* way, but surely... Surely it was an impossibility that after almost a year of trying she would finally fall pregnant when...

Alexandre felt a bit like his brain was short-circuiting. He couldn't seem to follow any thought to completion. It was all...*feeling*. Complex, confused, irrational *emotions*.

Surely she would have told him. If it was true, she would have returned. She would have *told* him.

And why the hell would she do that?

"What are you going to do?" Gabriel asked.

The question was asked with a gentleness Alexandre could not engage with. No one should be that gentle with a *king*. He was in charge. He was the one thing keeping everything together. So there could be no *gentle*.

Only decisions. Only leadership. Only moving forward with certainty and surety.

"I am going to this cabin, and I am going to bring her home."

"Alexandre, perhaps...perhaps you should let me or Gabriel do it." Evelyne smiled at him encouragingly, but he could see underneath that smile was a worry that he would not conduct himself as he should.

"I will be reasonable." Would Ines be? Well, she would have to be.

Reason was the only way out of this.

"Of course you will," Evelyne agreed, still with that kind of encouraging tone that made him want to grind his teeth together. "But it wouldn't hurt to have a friendly face—"

"I am her *husband*."

"Discuss what's going on before you—"

"Before I what?"

"Make demands and proclamations or say something you might regret."

You might regret. Like *he* was the problem here? "I am the king of Alis, Evelyne. Everything I do is a proclamation. I cannot regret this."

Evelyne sighed. "But you will," she muttered.

Alexandre ignored her. He went to his office. Then he stood there, frozen with an indecision that made it hard to breathe. He had to decide. He had to take charge. He had to *know* what was right or everything would crumble.

"If you're looking to do this under the radar, I can fly you."

Alexandre did not look behind him at the sound of Gabriel's voice. He couldn't face a man who knew him so well—who would read the panic when Alexandre could not allow *panic*.

So he would not consider Gabriel's words until he could *breathe*.

He had to breathe. Decide. Act. Protect. Ensure.

He blinked a few times, centering himself in the here and now. Ensuring he could speak clearly before he attempted it. "Yes. I will need to attend my meetings this afternoon." Because he could not shirk his duties, no matter the circumstance. "Can you get away early tomorrow morning?"

"Of course," Gabriel said.

He would act. Not regret his actions. He would go to this *cabin*, he would explain what would happen now— she would return to the palace, they would go back to the way things were, and now she had a child, likely, so there was no need for an annulment.

Everything could be as it should. It was a *relief*. The panic eased, but something else swept into its place. Because it struck him then, wholly and painfully. If she'd had a doctor come out three different times, she'd known.

She'd known and stayed away. Purposely. Not just

for a few days of adjusting to the information. She'd stayed away on purpose, knowing this truth, for *months*.

Why hadn't she come back? If the annulment request was just about having a child, and now she would have one, why would she stay away?

He rubbed at the pain in his chest and forced it down with the rest of his feelings. Deep under a wall of reason. Sense. *Action*.

It didn't matter why she'd stayed away. Because now it was time for her to come home.

Whether she wanted to or not. Whether he wanted her to or not. Everything would go back to the way it was, to the way he'd planned.

And that was that.

Ines had decided to wait for the second trimester. If the pregnancy was in good shape then, she would call Alexandre and inform him. She would lay out a plan where she stayed here. He didn't have to give her an annulment if that was a no go. He just had to let her *be*.

Because that was what she wanted. Or needed. Or something. She refused to allow herself to hope for some…change of heart from him just because she was pregnant. Because he did not want this, and *she* did.

So.

She made it into the second trimester in the sweet little cabin, enjoying the quiet days with Jonet, even if she was a bit bored without all her royal commitments. But she still replied to emails and sometimes even attended virtual meetings for some of her responsibilities. She missed going to meetings, visiting the orphanage and the children's hospital, the adaptive park she'd helped spearhead.

She tried not to think about Alexandre or the future and instead focused on caring for her changing body, her new home and her cousin.

When the doctor arrived for her four-month appointment, he went through the exam in the cabin as he had the past few times. They listened to the baby's heartbeat. He assured her everything was well.

Every time an appointment came, motherhood felt real and impending, and then the doctor would leave, and everything would feel like a dream again. Like she made it up.

But she was firmly in the second trimester of her pregnancy, which meant she needed to start planning for what happened on the *other* side of pregnancy. Which meant she needed to tell Alexandre, as she'd promised herself.

But she did not call Alexandre that night. She did not make plans to return to the palace. She knew it was wrong. Guilt swamped her every time she thought of him.

But so did fear. And anger. And a million other emotions.

When Ines crawled out of bed the next morning, tired and still vaguely nauseous, she figured she could give herself another month. Just to feel steadier. She didn't want to approach Alexandre when nausea still seemed to rule her life. She needed more...traction. Physically. Telling him in a month would be fair.

There was nothing he could do as a king or as a father at this stage in her pregnancy, so it wasn't *wrong*.

And if she still felt as emotionally confused and wrung out as she did now when the physical symptoms settled? Well, she would cross that bridge when she came to it.

She went into the kitchen hoping for some breakfast to soothe the unsteady feeling in her stomach, but Jonet stood in the living room, peering out the window.

She glanced at Ines over her shoulder. Grimaced. "Ines, we have a problem."

"What's that?" Ines moved over to the window, expecting to find some kind of wildlife conundrum. Instead, she saw a car parked in front of their cottage. It was black, sleek and *expensive*. It was certainly not the physician's car—their only visitor out all this way.

Then a familiar figure stepped out of the driver's side. He was dressed as casually as she'd *ever* seen him, like he was trying to fit in with the *commoners*. Jeans and a sweatshirt. Boots befitting the forest around them.

But there was nothing common about him. So tall. So *severe*. That preternatural control in everything he did—including striding toward the front door. Like he knew exactly what was on the other side.

He didn't *look* angry, but she knew he would have to be. If he was here, if he'd left his precious kingdom behind for even a moment… Yes, he was angry.

She had convinced herself if the king of Alis had not found her in all these months, he was not trying to find her. Had she been wrong? Had Jonet done such a good job of making them disappear that it had really taken him all this time to track her down?

She didn't know what to do with that thought, even

if her heart fluttered a bit. She didn't know what to do with *any* of this.

"Ines. Do you think he knows?"

Ines shook her head. If he knew, he'd... No, how could he possibly know if he was just showing up here now? "No. And he...he doesn't have to know," Ines heard herself say. Her body had changed *some*, but not much. He certainly wouldn't notice any thickening by the baggy clothes she wore.

She would send him away, and he wouldn't have to know. She could keep living in this space, where the baby was hers, and she did not have to deal with Alexandre's resentment.

"Ines, I'm not sure..." Jonet bit her lip. "You know I'll support you on anything. I'm on your side. But...he *is* your husband and the father of the baby. And, perhaps most importantly, a king."

The hard *rap* of knuckles on the door caused Ines to jump. She didn't have time to think. To plan.

"We can pretend we're not here," Jonet whispered.

For a moment, Ines held on to that thought. They could avoid this. All of this.

But this moment was a stark reminder that *hiding* did nothing but delay the inevitable. She could not pretend she wasn't here—because he was. She could not keep this pregnancy from him any longer—because it *existed*.

She had gotten her months of running away, wallowing, indulging in feelings and emotional responses, but she had known, deep down, that it could never be *real* life.

Not with a baby on the way.

So it was a crystalizing moment. Alexandre on the

other side of this door, knocking. Tracking her down. No doubt here to *fetch* her.

She'd run away thinking she was in charge. She wouldn't let him *control* her. She would live her life. For a while, it had felt like finding freedom after a lifetime of men controlling her.

But this wasn't living. It was hiding. It was avoiding the hard things because they hurt to deal with. If she wanted to build a life for herself, rather than go along with what she'd always been told, *hiding* was no answer. Maybe it was better than cowering or acquiescing, but it still wasn't what she wanted.

She wasn't fully sure *what* she wanted. Except to be a good mother. Something she'd never had. Her own mother had been negligent at best, dulling whatever pain she felt with alcohol or pills.

Hiding.

Ines would not hide and let her child deal with the fallout. No, she would always be the protector. The *mother*.

The pounding on the door started up again. Ines didn't flinch this time. It was time to make a choice. Time to start being a *mother*, not just a vessel.

"I'd like to speak to Alexandre alone, if you don't mind, Jonet."

"Of course. Shall I go to your room and pack your things?"

Ines inhaled deeply, let it out. "Yes, thank you."

CHAPTER SIX

ALEXANDRE HAD THOUGHT he'd braced himself for seeing Ines again. He had expected to feel a spurt of rage over what she was keeping from him, but he'd also expected some *time* to prepare. He'd *assumed* Jonet would answer the door.

Not his wife.

Her hair was pulled back, but not in her usual slick, elegant way. It was messy, strands falling out of the band. She wore something baggy and soft—not quite pajamas, but certainly not the kind of outfit a queen should wear in *public*.

It did nothing to undercut this moment of seeing her in the flesh for the first time in *months* and realizing how much he'd *missed* her. Looking at her across the dinner table. Listening to her chatter with Evelyne. The way she'd felt like such a seamless partner when they'd go over their schedules and determined who would handle what.

So for the past four months, essentially, he'd been alone again. Like before their engagement. When he'd felt his entire life was trying to mitigate his father's violent whims—toward Alis, toward Evelyne, toward Alexandre himself.

It had been quiet and empty, and he had never *realized* that his life was mostly made up of those two things—not until Ines had been there by his side for a year and then not at all.

He curled his hands into fists to keep from reaching out to touch her. Assuring himself she was real. That she was what he was missing.

Because he was missing nothing. He was a king. He had a kingdom to serve. His own wants mattered not at all. He was a king, not a husband. Not a man.

No matter what Ines made him feel sometimes.

He was missing *nothing*. Except a good night's sleep and the ability to be home, handling the responsibilities of his *kingdom*. Because of *her*.

"Good morning, Your Majesty," she said, with that old bland warmth that she'd trotted out before they were married. Sometimes even after. Like they were friends, but on a surface level. Acquaintances. Coworkers, maybe. She even gave a little curtsy.

He did not know what was wrong with him that it hit him like a bolt of lust. Luckily, anger swept in with it. That she could be so *casual*, with no sign of any kind of apology or even defiance.

Just *Good morning*, while everything inside of him raged and crashed around—emotion against bones. The only things keeping him from cracking apart were years of experience and the knowledge that emotional outbursts were the enemy.

Case. In. Point.

"So, to be clear, you disappear into thin air for nearly four months and you consider *Good morning, Your Majesty* the appropriate greeting?"

"Would you rather I be on my knees?"

He *knew* what she meant—begging forgiveness, but it was not the image in his head. No, that image was of his office and her on her knees for far different reasons.

She must have realized that, because her cheeks began to redden.

Which was *dangerous*. "We will return to the palace at once. Pack your bags." He braced himself for the argument—the anger, the emotion, the push and pull. He would not give in to it like he had three months ago. He would be strong, calm and cold in response to it.

He would be the *king* he had to be, not the man underneath that he could not be.

Jonet stepped out from somewhere in this rustic little cabin, carrying a collection of bags, pulling a suitcase behind her. "They are already packed."

Alexandre blinked. He looked from Jonet to Ines. Her expression was serene. For a moment, he had no words. She was just…agreeing with him? He thought there'd be refusals, arguments, shouts. Maybe even tears. She had stayed away all this time.

But she was just… She already had her bags packed.

He opened his mouth to say something, to question this, then thought better of it. Questioning could lead to an argument, and he wanted—needed—to avoid that.

He moved past Ines, doing everything he could not to touch her as he did, and approached Jonet.

She looked a little startled. "You don't need to—"

Over her objections, he relieved her of all the bags except the one she was pulling. He then carried said bags outside to his car, putting them in the trunk, not looking at the two women. He was just going to move forward as if he'd known all along they would follow his every command.

He *was* their king after all.

He opened the back-seat door for Jonet. She did *not* look comfortable. She shot Ines a questioning glance. Ines nodded her head regally, and Jonet slid inside the back seat. Ines made a move to follow, but Alexandre closed the door before she could. He moved to the passenger-side door, opened it and gestured her inside.

He watched the inner argument chase across her face. Be defiant, or go gently? He kept expecting defiance, but she simply slid into the passenger seat.

Since he did not know what to do with the ease at which this was going, he could only continue to move forward. He closed her door, then got into the driver's seat.

Ines was frowning at him. "You're driving?"

He glanced at her. "Yes."

She looked away. "How modern," she murmured.

Modern. He felt about as modern as a caveman at the moment. But he drove away from her little cabin, away from her betrayal, and back to the private airport Gabriel had arranged for him to fly in and out of without detection, something that could be done with Gabriel piloting the plane himself.

Gabriel must have been surprised at their quick arrival, though he did not say anything. He simply greeted Ines and Jonet and helped Alexandre load the bags onto the plane while the women settled themselves into their seats.

Everything continued to go easily. They flew back to Alis. Gabriel drove them back to the palace. Gabriel took Ines's and Jonet's bags. The staff knew they had been gone, but the more they handled this clandestinely, the more whatever stories Alexandre came up with to explain the past few months would be believable.

He dismissed Jonet to return to her own quarters. He said nothing to Ines. Ines said nothing to him. But they both walked through the palace to their residential wing.

As they began to approach her set of rooms, she walked in front of him. Down the hall toward her door. As though she was just going to go inside, go back to their old lives, without a peep.

He should rejoice at that. In fact, the entire trip back he'd conceived a plan to let it all go. Let it play out. See what she did. See how she handled all this. He'd determined it was the best course of action to simply *let things be*.

She reached her door, lifted a hand to the doorknob, but he couldn't keep the words inside. All his plans fell to ash around him, just like always seemed to happen when it came to her.

"When were you planning on telling me?"

She stopped, her hand frozen on the doorknob. For a moment, she said nothing, keeping her back to him. Stiff. *Caught*. But she did not give in right away. "Telling you what?"

"That you are pregnant."

Ines stood there in the hall, her back to Alexandre, heart beating hard against her ribs.

He knew. *How* did he know? How could he have found that out? Certainly not by *looking* at her. Perhaps she was heavier than she had been, her curves a bit more pronounced, but she wore clothes that hid that, she was almost certain.

"Unless you are sick, and that is the reason for these monthly doctor's appointments, but you certainly do not look *ill*."

She inhaled, trying to work through that. So he didn't know for *sure*, but he knew a doctor had been to see her... And suddenly it all made sense. It wasn't that he *hadn't* found her for months and now suddenly had.

He'd known where she was. Known everything. He simply hadn't *collected* her for all these months. She closed her eyes, surprised at how much that realization hurt. Almost as bad as his never looking for her in the first place. He knew, and he hadn't come to fetch her, fight for her or even let her go. He'd just...kept watch.

"You were just...keeping tabs on me all this time?" Why did she sound so winded? How could she be so hurt? She *knew* him. Of course he had been doing just that. Why had she expected different?

"I could hardly let my queen gallivant off unprotected."

"Gallivant?" She laughed bitterly, turning to face him. She leaned against the door behind her and studied him. "I ran away from you, Alexandre."

If he had any reaction to this, it was hidden behind that forbidding expression. "You did not do a very good job," he said flatly. Just standing there, somehow looking regal in his casual attire. Looking disapproving and detached.

Because he'd known for all this time where she'd been. He hadn't come to fetch her until he'd heard there was a *doctor* involved. A *child* involved.

"Answer the question, Ines," he ordered, as he always did, with complete certainty his order would be followed. It was funny how even now it didn't prompt her to want to be contrary for the sake of it. His demand for the truth was a fair-enough one, and she didn't have energy for anything other than the truth.

"When was I planning on telling you? I don't know. I promised myself I would after the three-month appointment. And then I gave myself another month to feel more…to be stronger. Physically. Being pregnant is not for the faint of heart."

She saw a flicker of worry cross his face. Watched as he took a few steps toward her and then stopped as if remembering himself.

How could these two polarities exist inside him? Worry and kindness and warmth versus that cold, demanding detachment.

King and real man underneath? Mask and truth? It didn't feel that easy. There was something messier at play, and she wanted to dive in and not fix it—there was no fixing the complications of humanity—she simply wanted to understand. To make sense of him.

"But you are well," he said, his voice a little rough. He phrased this like a statement, like she had to be well because he said so.

But it *was* a question, no matter how he put it. And it softened her when it shouldn't. Like it might concern him that she was well. That this was not a totally one-sided connection, no matter how much he might like it to be.

"I am well. The baby is well."

His gaze dropped, just for a fleeting moment, to her

stomach. He could not see the soft swell of her belly under the draping of her shirt, she knew, but she felt *seen* just the same.

"We have much to discuss," Alexandre said roughly, then made no move to discuss it.

"Yes, I suppose we do, but I am tired. And hungry."

"I shall have a tray sent up. Some breakfast cake and tea. That's usually what you prefer this time of day, yes?"

"Yes." She stared at him, wondering if it was foolish to be touched that he knew that about her, or was it his robotic need to make everything *correct*? To know what she ate and when. Was it control? Interest? Concern?

Maybe it was all three. Maybe his feelings for her were as mixed up as hers were for him. Because she should be angry and defiant and contrary, and she *did* feel some anger. But she also ached to touch him.

She'd *missed* him. His steady presence. He was such an *anchor*, even when they were doing little more than sharing a meal, she felt safe with him. In ways that were new to her because growing up in her father's house had always meant being concerned how she would be used next.

Alexandre didn't *use* her. Even when he was controlling, even when he was so worried about their *optics* and his kingdom. She wasn't a pawn so much as a useful *tool*, and that meant he valued her in some way.

But he frustrated her and concerned her and infuriated her and… And he was standing close enough right now that she just wanted to kiss him. To feel what she'd felt in his office all those months ago. An uncontrollable heat—something so big, so important, so soul-deep that even perfect, controlled King Alexandre couldn't resist.

Because now she knew there *was* some hidden Achilles' heel to him. Was it her? Was it anger? She didn't know. The only thing she knew for certain was that for a year she'd held back. And when she finally hadn't, she'd gotten what she wanted. Because she wanted this baby with all she was—*regardless* of him.

But he was still a factor, because she wanted to touch him. And she was done pretending she didn't. Done holding herself back.

Like Jonet had said back at the cabin, now it was about what *she* wanted.

So she stepped across the space between them, moved to her toes and pressed her mouth to his. Just because she could. Just because she wanted to.

She'd come back with no promises. Which meant this return was like…a fresh start. Not the clinical agreement they'd made when they'd married. No, she was someone else now.

So this time around, she was going to take what she wanted.

And for one sweet, blissful moment, he kissed her back with such *desperation* she could almost believe he'd missed her as she'd missed him. That there was something between them—an emotional connection they could work through, they could grow and tend to. Believe in.

A moment, a *flash* of that hope and joy, but he locked it down and away quickly this time.

His hands curled around her upper arms, and then

she was being pulled away. Put back. His gaze was hard, even if she could see the unsteady rise and fall of his chest.

"You will behave yourself now that you are home, Ines."

It made her angry, but there was something more than anger now. She looked up at him, feeling like crying. Why would he kiss her like that and then push her away? Why was it all push then pull? Why did none of it make sense?

"I don't understand you."

For a moment, so clear and intent, she saw exactly why in his eyes.

For a strange, disorienting moment—likely for both of them—she saw clearly that he didn't understand himself.

But that was quickly swept away, into ice and distance and control.

"Get your rest, Ines. Your food will be up shortly. Try not to run away again. It will not be tolerated a second time, particularly while you carry my child."

My child. How did he pull her in two totally different directions? Love and affection and *care* that he didn't know himself, that he tried so hard to be good. And a cold, cutting fury that he could say things like that to her.

My child. When he hadn't even wanted a child. He'd wanted an *heir*, until he hadn't needed one. And then he'd…cut her off. Cut himself off. And she could believe that it was this simple. He didn't want her.

But he *did*. He kissed her like a man starving. The

way they'd come together, angry and wild, those months ago was not an uninterested man.

It was a tortured one.

The way he strode away now, quick and purposeful, was a bit like a man chased by *something*.

So maybe it was that... It wasn't the child, the pregnancy. It was her. He *wanted* her but didn't want to. He *felt* this thing between them but wanted to control it.

Because it was uncontrollable. Because it was unpredictable. Because it did not fit into the neat little order of his life he'd created trying to be the antithesis of his father, the savior of his country and his people.

But he was Alexandre, so he didn't understand *middle ground*. He had been raised by a monster, and while he had somehow turned out good in spite of it, he didn't understand his own humanity.

Which meant Ines knew what she needed to do now.

CHAPTER SEVEN

ALEXANDRE IMMEDIATELY WENT back to work once he'd ordered Ines a tray of her preferred morning snack.

He had *wanted* to track down the doctor who'd checked out Ines and demand to know every detail. It seemed a better action item than standing there cataloging all the ways her body had slightly changed in all these months.

Better than wondering how he'd lost control of all this and wanting to beg her forgiveness for wrongs he *hadn't* committed.

Because he was a king, and he was right. *She* was in the wrong. No matter how at ease she seemed with *everything*, down to growing a child.

A child. *Their* child. His child.

He was to be a father, and he knew what that meant: be the opposite his father in every way. But he didn't know what that meant in terms of being a *king*—his most important role. His *only* role.

Except Ines had upended all of that. Pregnant. Growing a child. So many dangers in that simple, age-old cycle.

But she'd said she was well. The baby was well. And

Ines was not like his mother. She had no reasons to hide the truth of her health from him like his mother had hidden the truth from his father. Leading directly to her death during labor.

Sometimes Alexandre thought of that and wondered if she'd signed her own death sentence on purpose. Just to escape. Just to leave it all to *him*.

And since he was thinking about *that* awful time, and apparently blaming his poor victimized mother for anything, he kept his afternoon appointments, conferred with his assistant over a few requests and approved various action items. He skipped lunch and got out of his head, out of his past *and* his future, and into the present.

Until it was time for dinner. Something he might have skipped too, but he was not a coward. Ines was back, and everything would go back to the way it was. If it did, he would know how to handle this new role she'd thrust upon him.

Which meant he would not *hide*.

If he could get through to Ines to stop kissing him and such, everything would be *fine*.

Besides, he'd stopped that, hadn't he? Perhaps it had been difficult to set her away instead of sink into her, hold on tight and assure himself she was real and back and *here* and that meant all was well.

All *would* be well. Without kissing. Without any changes. They would go back to the way things had been. She'd had her time to run away, and she'd gotten the child she'd wanted. There was no reason for anything to change. She would be a mother. He would be a king. Easy.

So why did his heart beat in odd, anxious flutters in his chest as he walked to the dining room this evening?

Ines sat at the table—not in her usual seat, but everything else about the scene was usual. Her hair was sleekly pulled back instead of haphazard. She wore a dress more befitting her station. She did not wear the earrings he'd given her as a wedding present, or the necklace she usually wore on casual days without appointments, but she was wearing his ring.

Because everything was back the way it should be, or so he kept assuring himself. But Alexandre did not know how to get rid of this unease sitting on his chest. She was giving him exactly what he wanted. Returning everything back to normal, *just as it should be*.

He couldn't seem to relax and trust that this was true. Which was when he started to pick up on that which was *not* normal. Like the fact that table was only set for two—right next to each other.

"Where are Evelyne and Gabriel?"

Ines studied him for a moment before answering. "They are eating in their rooms this evening."

"That is highly unusual." He studied the table arrangement. He did not want to sit *right* next to her. They usually sat across from each other. But she was next to *his* seat, and it was set for him, and...

"I asked for some privacy as we discuss what's next."

His gaze went from the table setting to her. "What do you mean, *what's next*?"

"How things will go on now that I am pregnant."

"Nothing will change. Everything will go back to the way it was, except we will now follow the plans we'd previously made for a child. You will scale back your old responsibilities of course, but for the most part, everything goes on as it was."

She sighed. "Yes, I had a feeling you'd say that." She shook her head. "This does not work for me."

"I beg your pardon?"

She sighed. "Sit, Alexandre."

He balked at being told what to do, but a staff member appeared with the first course, and Alexandre had no choice, he felt, but to take the seat next to Ines. To continue on as normal for *him*, even if she was determined to make things difficult.

She gave his hand a little pat as the course was served, like she was *placating him*.

"I have missed the palace food," she said, smiling as the bowl of soup was put in front of her. "Jonet has kitchen skills I do not possess, but nothing like this."

Just normal conversation after saying their *plans* did not work for her—even though she'd been a part of making them. Or, at least, agreeing to them.

Once the staff had left them to the first course, Ines spoke again.

"We have only a few months between now and when the baby is born. For those next months, we will do the following." She picked up one of the portfolio-notebook combinations she was always using for business. He hadn't noticed it there on the other side of her, but now she handed it to him.

He took it.

She began to eat, so he opened it and saw a list in Ines's beautifully perfect handwriting. Neat. Organized.

Alarming.

Because as he read everything in her neatly printed list, his unease grew.

On weekends, we will eat meals together privately, in our own quarters, unless there is an event. They had never eaten meals together *privately*. They always ate here—with or without guests or his sister.

We will walk the gardens once a day together—you may have your assistant schedule a time or choose spontaneously. Spontaneously? He was trying to rebuild a *country*, and she wanted him to accompany her on *walks*.

We will return to our appointment schedule—with the additional requirement you spend the night in my bed on such evenings.

"What is this?" he demanded, frustrated that even *reading* the word *appointment* seemed to elicit a physical response in his body.

"Well, this is what normal married people do, Alexandre. They have private time together. They are intimate. They build a relationship outside of their roles in public. I realize we are not normal, and it occurred to me that you might need spelled out for you what I require to remain in this marriage."

Remain? "You are pregnant. You are the queen. There is no getting out of this marriage, Ines." He closed the portfolio and handed it back to her, but she did not take it. "You made certain of that whether you wanted to or not."

She held his gaze calmly, even as he felt the scalding heat of frustration poke at him.

"These are my terms, Alex. This is what the next few months will entail if you'd like me to stay put."

Alex. Alex. Why did it matter if she shortened his name? Why did it feel like she was talking to some version of himself he wished existed but didn't?

He cleared his throat, forced himself to focus. "And if I do not agree to this plan?"

"I will continue to run away," she said evenly, her gaze direct. "Every chance I get. You will have to lock me in a dungeon to stop me."

"And you think I won't?"

"No. I don't. You'll want to, God knows." She put down her spoon, took a sip of water. "But it will remind you of your father. And you won't be able to go through with it."

"You'd be surprised."

"No, Alex, I wouldn't be," she said, with absolutely no hesitation. "You have too much nobility in you to ever sink to your father's levels in anything more than thought."

"Perhaps I just haven't been pushed far enough yet."

She watched him, that blue gaze of hers as steady as ever. When she spoke, each word somehow felt like a curse. "If you haven't yet, you never will be."

The staff of course chose that moment to clear the first course and replace it with the second. Alexandre sat there in a seething silence, trying to get ahold of his temper.

If you haven't yet, you never will be.

He did not know how to believe that was true, but she said it so matter-of-factly, as if there was no doubt.

Once they were alone again, she kept prattling on in between greedy bites.

"Nevertheless, I will take that chance. If you refuse to abide by my rules, I will involve the press. I will embarrass you, if I must. But if you agree to my terms, and the baby comes and nothing has changed—you have no feelings for me, want nothing from me except to be some excellent queen mannequin—I will release you from my horrible attempts to give us a real marriage. I will go back to the way things were, remain as your wife, your queen, the mother of your child in this detached, joyless, loveless abyss."

He could only stare at her. *Detached, joyless, loveless abyss?* Is that how she saw her life? It felt like something banded around his lungs and squeezed. It felt like *guilt*—when he'd never promised her anything but just what she laid out.

"But you must give me a chance first."

"A chance for what?" he asked, truly baffled by this woman who had been *perfect* for nearly a year and over the past few months had taken all that perfection and ease away.

She cocked her head, studying him. "To show you what living feels like."

Living. What else did he do every day but live? Meet all his lofty goals, turn this country back into what it could be? "I breathe. I live."

"You breathe. You *exist*. You deserve more. *I* deserve more. Our baby deserves more."

He could not even grasp these words.

"So do you agree?" she asked. She had cleared her plate. He had not touched his food.

Agree? He could not agree to this. It was pointless. A waste of time. It was…a ransom of sorts, and he did not deal with terrorists anymore, now that his father was dead.

But he *did* have experience with these kinds of tests, didn't he? Hoops to jump through to prove himself. His father had given him nothing but tests and hoops and challenges. Of course, there'd been no winning those.

He could win this one. Ines was honest and fair, even if this was utterly ridiculous. She wouldn't change the stakes.

What was a few months? She would be pregnant the entire time, and if he could suffer through these months of her pretending they could be more than their roles, their titles, their *responsibility*, on the other side of it was everything he wanted.

A partnership with his queen. A detached, joyless, loveless abyss as she defined it. Yes, *that* was what he wanted.

And she would have her child—the best doctors in the world would ensure she and the baby were healthy through this—so she would get what *she* wanted.

And all would be well.

He just had to resist his wife through a few months of *intimacy*. He'd survived nearly a year before. He could do this. He would do this.

For Alis. Even for *her*, though she would not see it that way.

Ines thought her acting was superb this evening. Alexandre had to believe she was nonchalant and unaffected.

That she would happily trot away to wreak havoc on his life if he did not agree to her terms.

She *would* do it, but it would hurt. Even when she was furious with him, she would take no joy in trying to ruin his reputation. He cared so much for it, and she understood why. She didn't want to continue to run or go to the press.

She wanted what she'd outlined. A *marriage*.

And it had occurred to her, after she'd eaten her morning cake and taken that long nap this afternoon, that he didn't even know what that might look like. If he didn't know himself, didn't understand his own feelings, then why should he know what a functioning relationship looked like? His only example was likely his parents—and while Alex almost never mentioned his mother, knowing King Enzo meant Ines knew it could not have been good.

Not that she had any fine example of marriage in her life, but she had solid relationships that weren't romantic. With Jonet. With Evelyne. She understood how to care for someone without needing to protect them. Without the threat and terror of abuse in every corner.

Alexandre loved his sister. He even loved Gabriel. He was *capable* of love, but Ines did not think he understood it except in the role of protector or savior. He only knew how to exist in a world where people owed him for being the good one in relation to the evil one— King Enzo.

With his father dead, he was only protecting everyone from his memory. Something no one needed. Especially her. He did not need to be her protector in anything, so he did not know what to do with her except keep her at arm's length.

There would be no more arm's length. She was sure—*almost certain*—that if she could get him to behave as a real husband, as though they were in a real relationship, he would see that it was possible. Neither he nor his kingdom would crumble if he was allowed to be the real man underneath the cold, detached crown.

"Fine. I agree to your terms. Dinners. Appointments. Et cetera." He waved these away like they were inconsequential.

But they wouldn't be. Ines wouldn't allow them to be. She beamed at him, showing only her pleasure that she'd won—not the wave of relief that he hadn't made her hurt them both by running away over and over again. "Excellent."

When dessert was served, she ate her fill. A well of hunger had begun to displace the nauseous feeling. *Or you're just happy to be home.*

She looked around the luxurious dining room full of history—some of its furnishings particularly ugly—and did not know for sure when it had begun to feel like home. Early on, she supposed, when she'd decided that marrying Alexandre meant marrying Alis, meant marrying his *goals*.

If she could be a good queen, if she could belong to and serve Alis, then she could be something. More than the pawn her father had used her as.

But she wanted to be more than a useful tool now. She wanted to be a person too. Who loved her husband and her child. Who had a family. They would always be beholden to their country, but they all deserved a place to go to just be themselves.

She would have to build it, to show Alexandre it was possible.

With dinner finished, Alexandre stood and helped her up out of her chair as he always did. But she did not let his hand go. "Shall we take our garden walk? And then, tonight would be our normal appointment, would it not?"

He stiffened, as she'd known he would. He even cleared his throat. "Surely you are exhausted from your travel."

"Funny how a short drive and an equally short flight on a private plane did not quite exhaust me. Besides, I took a nap between lunch and dinner. Do you have any other excuses you'd like to trot out?"

His face became a storm. "They are not excuses, Ines."

"Then what are they?" she asked, feigning innocence.

But he had no answer for that. Just a disapproving expression. "Very well," he muttered. "We will go for our walk."

She noted he did not mention their *appointment*, but she let that slide for now. He tucked his arm into hers and led her out of the dining room, through the palace, and then out one of the terrace doors that would lead them down to the gardens.

The night was warm, the scent of flowers and midnight wafting around them. The gardens were extensive and one of Ines's favorite places in the palace. Some long-gone ancestor of Alexandre's had planted them, and the gardeners tended them, and in every season there were different delights to discover if a person perused the winding, meandering pathways.

Ines often did just that, alone, instead of with her husband. But tonight, they walked, her arm tucked into Alexandre's, and she felt something ease inside of her that had been tied tight these past four months.

Perhaps she'd known all along that running away wasn't the answer, but she was glad she'd done it. Learned something from it. And now she was glad to be back, fighting for something good.

"This reminds me of our wedding."

"Why?"

The bafflement in his tone made her smile, because the memory was not *with* him. It was before. "My hair and makeup was done, but they hadn't put me in that monstrosity of a dress yet."

She watched his face illuminated by moonlight, surprised to see his mouth curve ever so slightly. "It was a bit of a monstrosity."

Neither of them had been allowed any say in it. Their wedding had not been for *them*. It had been for King Enzo to show off his wealth—well, her father's wealth combining with the king's power. But still, they had said vows, married and consummated said marriage.

And here they were over a year later. Walking the gardens. A baby on the way. It should be enough, but it wasn't. Not yet.

"I needed some air while they dealt with how they were going to get me into such a thing. So I came out here. I sat there on that bench and looked at the gardens.

I listened to the birds. I told myself that it didn't matter if I hadn't chosen this, there were things I could choose. Like being a leader and a good princess. That even if your father was a scary monster, there was…you."

He eyed her warily as they walked through an archway of blooming trees.

"Do you know what I thought when I first met you?" she asked him. Because they never discussed *them*. They never discussed anything but work, and that needed to change.

He did not say anything, and that slight curve to his mouth flattened.

She kept talking. He would not silence her. "You were so handsome, but so severe. And I had no reason to trust my father's choice in suitor, and, of course, I knew what a despot your father was. Even though people around the palace seemed to speak highly of you, I could hardly take it at their word. And then we met in that reception room. Do you remember?"

The wariness in his expression had only intensified. "Yes."

"And what did you think of me?"

He took a moment, no doubt searching for the *right* answer in his mind, not the actual answer. "That you were very small."

She rolled her eyes. "Are you always looking for ways to protect, Alex?"

Something flickered in his eyes. She was beginning to think he actually *liked* it when she shortened his name. Few people did it. Evelyne or Gabriel sometimes, but not often.

The longer name suited who he was better, but there was a man inside who was more than his long, royal name.

"You were very polite. We talked of birds. Do you remember? I said I liked birds—just a nervous blurt because you were being so silent and foreboding—but then you spoke, and you very kindly told me there were great places to watch birds in the gardens."

His gaze lowered to hers, his eyebrows furrowed as if he didn't quite understand what she was saying.

"And then the next time I came, you showed me. Every time, you always looked after my comfort. You were always gentle. Nothing in my life had ever been *gentle* before. Pampered, yes, but not gentle. Does that make sense?"

He looked at her, not detached now. Maybe a little confused. He didn't answer, but she thought it did make sense to him. She thought if anyone could understand the difference it was him.

"I went into those first few meetings with you always waiting you to show your true colors. But after a while, I began to understand. You were different than the men I'd known in my life. Not perfect, certainly. Abrupt and aloof and…cold, at times. But you had a goal—to see your kingdom and your sister survive your father. And to be nothing like him. And when I realized that, I began to trust you."

Alexandre stopped—not quite abruptly, but the stop wasn't smooth either. "We should return. You do not want to overdo it."

"A walk is hardly overdoing anything." But she let

him lead her back inside. Up to their wing. She could feel the stiffness enter his body, like knots tying in slow succession—tighter and tighter, until he stopped at her door.

He opened his mouth, no doubt to dismiss her. To find some excuse to put her off.

But this was the deal.

She opened the door to her set of rooms, curled her other hand in his sleeve so she could pull him in behind her.

He could have stopped. He was certainly bigger and stronger than her, but he didn't pull back. Still, he looked uncomfortable as she closed the door behind him. Like he didn't want to be here.

But here he was. He had *agreed* to this.

In the past, whenever he'd arrived for one of their *appointments*, it was usually late. She was usually already in bed…waiting, waiting, waiting. She'd always let him set the tone, and he'd always set it…carefully.

Seen to her pleasure, his. It had been enjoyable, but it had not been like that day in his office because they had both known what it was about. Not pleasure. Not enjoyment. Not intimacy.

An heir.

This was different. It would be different. This was them—beyond their roles and their masks. Though, he would try to hold tight to his.

She faced him now, in the entry of her rooms. He stood stiffly. But stiff wouldn't do.

So she wrapped her arms around his neck. His expression was cool, but she knew she just needed to learn where to look. He was *not* passionless. He was *not* unaffected. She would find the signal somewhere in him.

But right now, she would keep talking. She would talk and talk and talk. Let all those scary truths inside of her out until he saw her, until he trusted her enough to show himself. His true self.

"I was terrified of our wedding night," she said, reveling in the feel of pressing her soft body to his hard one.

"Ines."

It was a warning, but she was done heeding his warnings. "But you were gentle and kind. You promised you would do everything in your power not to hurt me, and I believed you. Because you had shown me nothing but kindness."

"Yes, kind. I am kind. I get the picture."

She laughed at the disgust in his voice. Because he was so many things aside from kind, but that was what had allowed her to find some *ease* in this marriage in the beginning. "I was so relieved. You could have been anything." She moved to her toes, pressed a light kiss to his mouth. "Cruel." She kissed his chin. "Abusive." The corner of his mouth. "Arrogant and cutting." She kissed him on the mouth, deeper this time, and his arms came around her. "Dismissive. Horrible. You could have smelled like rotted fish."

"I am a *king*, Ines."

She smiled against his mouth. "You were a prince at the time, and I'm quite sure both could smell awful if they've a mind to. But you don't. And didn't. You were something *good*, and I promised myself in that moment that no matter what difficulties we faced, I would be grateful for that."

His hold tightened for a moment, and not in any kind of sensual way. "So grateful you ran away?" he demanded gruffly. A little flare of temper in his eyes.

The edge in him thrilled her. She knew how hard he worked to keep that temper hidden. That she could bring it out meant something.

It simply *had* to mean something.

"The thing is you can't live your life being grateful for crumbs. This is something I only began to realize when I saw there is more out there to have, more than just roles and games and being someone else's pawn. I came to realize I wanted so much more than the crumbs."

"You are a *queen*, Ines."

"Yes, I am your queen." She stepped back, trying not to grin when it clearly took him a minute to realize he needed to release her. When he did, she reached for the hem of her dress. It was a soft, stretchy fabric, easily pulled up and over her head.

His eyes raked over her as she dropped the dress to the floor, though he stayed stiff and still and where he was. A statue. A crown.

But underneath that beat the heart of a *man*. She wanted to show it to him. Again and again and again, until she got through to him. It would take time. He'd spent years building these walls. Hardening his heart. Protecting himself just as much as he protected everyone else.

But she had time. Months. She would get through

to him. Not just for herself. Not just for Alexandre. For their baby. For their *family*.

"I have no regrets, Alexandre. You have been more than I could have ever hoped for when my father said he had found me a husband." She crossed to him, reached up and began to unbutton his shirt.

"Why are you trying to make me out to sound—"

"Good? Noble?" She met his gaze.

His breath shuddered out as her hands slid over the expanse of skin she'd exposed by unbuttoning his shirt. "Yes. That."

She pressed a kiss to the underside of his jaw. Always in search of some spot he might have missed with his ruthless razor. But he was always perfect, wasn't he? She let her hands explore the hard, tense muscles of his chest and abdomen. "Because you are both. You are also bad and selfish. And obnoxious and bossy. And honorable beyond reason. Handsome. Strong."

"Ines." He caught her wrists with his hands.

She looked up at him. "Because we're all a mess of lots of things, don't you think?"

His gaze was hard, his jaw clenched tight. "I most assuredly do *not*."

She smiled at him, even though he was disagreeing with her. Because he was wrong, and she would *prove it*.

"If we are to do this," he muttered, pulling her hands off his chest, "let us go to your bed."

She shook her head. "No. No, I don't think so. I know how that goes."

His eyebrows drew together, as if he honestly didn't know what she meant by that.

"You turn off the lights. You try to turn off…everything. Just get the job done." She took his palm, pressed it against her stomach. "The job's been done. This, tonight, and for the next few months isn't a *job*. It is just us."

"It is an action item on your to-do list, Ines." He said it with his trademark cool disdain, but his warm palm remained on her stomach. And in his eyes, she saw that hint of something…hot over cold. Intent instead of detachment.

So she moved his hand down, to touch her where she ached for him. His gaze followed his hand, and then she did not need to guide it because he stroked, over the fabric of her underwear but exactly where she wanted to be touched.

Yes, she had missed this. The fires he could stoke within her. Because he was relentless in all things, even this. His fingers slid under the fabric to find her. The core of her. He knew just where to touch, where to apply pressure, how to find that first, throbbing peak.

She held on to his shoulders, her body a shuddering mass of what he always brought her. But he was still standing there in control. Maybe there was the flicker of something triumphant in his dark gaze. Maybe she could see the outline of his arousal against his pants. But she had not broken through that wall.

She would. She *would*. There was no point to being back here, to accepting that her runaway had done *nothing*, if she did not get through to him.

"Come, Ines." It was not the dirty order she might like. He was trying to lead her to the bedroom. He wanted lights off, heart off, and she *refused*. So she did not let herself be pulled.

She unbuttoned and unzipped his pants quickly. She was trembling and desperate for more. More of him. More of everything. Once she managed to get his clothes off him, she pulled him to the ground. Here in the pretty sitting room she took appointments in. The light on. So she could see him. The ridges of muscle that tensed, contracted, jerked under her hands. Under her body as she straddled him.

His breath was ragged, but there was still distance in his eyes. It faltered when she gripped him, guided him to her. She wanted to see more than a falter. She wanted an obliteration.

So she moved against him in shallow, teasing strokes, not meant to do anything more than stir.

A hand came to her hip, clamped down, pulling her so that she had to sink down, sighing in contented pleasure to be filled by him once more. To be *here*, fighting for something rather than running away from all he couldn't give her. And if he never did—

She stopped that thought in its tracks. She would only think in positives. And for now, the positive was the pleasure wrapping around her body. The intimacy of two bodies moving with the same purpose.

Intimacy—except, he was holding himself back. He was being so *careful*. Yes, he would give her pleasure. Yes, he would find his own. But there was that old wall between them. Like they were *only* bodies, nothing more.

She could not abide it. Not now that she knew there

was some part of him that she could find if she broke down that wall.

She leaned forward, pressing her body to his, even with him lodged deep inside her. She pressed a kiss to his mouth, then dragged her lips to his ear.

"You do not have to be anyone but yourself with me," she murmured there, before nipping at the lobe with her teeth. "Gentle. Rough. Sweet. Dirty. Whatever you are, I want that, Alex. Because *I* am yours."

CHAPTER EIGHT

IT WAS AN ONSLAUGHT. Too many emotions, feelings, sensations. Too much *her*. There were proclamations he'd given himself, and he didn't know where they disappeared to.

Because it wasn't like the last time. It wasn't *wild* per se. It wasn't frustration bubbling over.

I am yours.

How he wanted her to be. Needed her to be. Couldn't *let* her be.

But she was moving against him, soft and sweet. It didn't have to be about her words. It was two bodies. That was how he'd always seen it. How he'd prepared himself every time he'd come to her room. That this act was separate from who they were and what they must do.

Nothing felt separate, and all his old proclamations to himself were deserting him. She was making it so difficult to hold on to them. To separate duty from need. Because there was no duty here now. She *was* pregnant. So this was all…something else. He could not pretend it was duty. He *wanted* it to be proof that he did not need such soft things.

But in the moment, he felt as though he needed her or he might never breathe again. All those careful fortifications that kept him separate, that kept him protected, that kept him *sane* felt more of a burden than necessary when she nipped at his ear. When she said those things. When she shuddered and came apart around him with his name on her lips.

He moved up, tangling his hands in his hair to find that wildness that was dangerous and he should avoid, but with her it only felt elemental.

You do not have to be anyone but yourself with me.

It was a dangerous, insidious thought. Too good to be true. Things that felt this good were only ever harbingers of doom.

She met every thrust, every wild desperate move with one of her own. She used her teeth on his bottom lip, and he emptied himself in a shuddering, mind-blanking moment that seemed to echo on and on until he collapsed onto the floor.

A *floor*. In a room where she took appointments with palace staff. In a room not meant for *this*. But she snuggled in, her head tucked into his shoulder, her naked body tangled with his. She had a *smile* on her face.

On her floor. While she carried his child. No, this would not do.

He bundled her up in his arms. She made a low, contented sound in her throat that was both a dagger to his heart, and a salve to some part of him he tried to ignore existed. He carried her through the doorway to her sitting room, then another door to her bedchamber.

It was dim in the room, but he had navigated it in

the dark every time he'd come for one of their *appointments*, so he knew the way.

He deposited her in her bed, ready to leave, *needing* to leave, but she held out her hand as if to invite him into her bed. Because he was meant to stay, when he had never once allowed himself that before. To stay here in warmth and sated pleasure was akin to taking some kind of drug. He couldn't allow it.

But it was on her list. A list he'd agreed to. Because he would prove to her this changed nothing. *Nothing.* So he got into the bed, and she curled up against him again.

Perhaps it was the deal, but if she fell asleep… Well, he had every right to leave, didn't he? He'd tell her he was called away. That she did not get to have first dibs on a *king*. He could go along with some of her little list, but not all. Not all the time. Just enough to hold up his end of the bargain, but not enough so that she *won*.

He'd just wait until she slept, and then he would slip out. Everything would be—

But the next thing he knew, he woke up with his wife in his arms and morning light filtering into the room.

He looked down at her sleeping form and wondered if letting her run away again—or throwing her in the dungeons—might be a better option.

Because he did not want to get out of bed. He was tempted to stay right here, watching the morning light gild her beautiful face. He wanted to feel the soft, even rise and fall of her chest.

You do not have to be anyone but yourself with me.

What a ridiculous statement. Because he always had to be a king. He always had to be a man who would put his country above his ego. And what was this damnable lust except some version of ego? Selfish desires. This *yearning* was all the things he'd taught himself to reject.

He slid out of bed. He was careful to be quiet, collecting his clothes and pulling them on. With each item of clothing, he managed to build back a layer of armor. Of *kingly duty*. Maybe these months would not be so bad.

If he could wake up and find King Alexandre again… he could survive this. Give her what she wanted, then the baby would be here, and she would have that. She would not have a need for…this.

Everything would work out all right. He would make as certain of that as he did everything else.

"Good morning," he heard her murmur, sounding sleepy and satisfied. He didn't dare turn around to see what that looked like on her face. He had met her demands, and now he would get a respite from them.

"You will meet with the palace doctors after breakfast," he said, sounding stiff and formal to his own ears. "You will follow all their directives."

She didn't say anything at first, and he didn't dare look at her, though he could hear the rustle of sheets, the sound of feet meeting the carpet. "Your health is paramount," he continued, pulling on the rest of his clothes. "You will not hide anything from them. Pregnancy and childbirth is a dangerous time for a woman, if you are not aware."

He felt her approach but did not look. Had she pulled on clothes or something to cover herself with? Was she naked? How much time could he spare to tumble her back into that bed and—

No. They had *appointments* for a reason. Lines. Boxes. Carefully constructed protections.

"I hadn't thought..." She trailed off, somewhere behind him. She didn't say anything else.

"Hadn't thought what?" he demanded, feeling irritation scratch along his skin.

She slid her hands down his back, then around him, hugging him from behind. Her cheek pressed to his spine. "I *knew* your mother died in childbirth, but I did not really put it together. That you were old enough to understand what was going on. That it might have marked you."

He froze. When he spoke, he felt as brittle as thin ice. "It did not mark me. It simply made me aware that pregnancy can be a dangerous time if one does not take care of themself."

"You were so tense the day Evelyne went into labor. So...wound tight. It's why you lost control, no doubt. You were terrified."

He had not considered...but that was ridiculous. Yes, he had some concern for his sister, and learning that morning that she had gone into labor had left him worried. But only because she'd been away for so much of her pregnancy and had dealt with some stress during it. That didn't mean he was...*terrified*.

"I will go to whatever doctor's appointments you like. And I will give them permission to tell you everything."

He pulled her arms off him, stepped away and fixed a glare on his face. "Ines, I am—"

"The king, yes, I know." She was wearing a brief, silky robe that covered enough...and yet not enough, because he wanted to rid her of it immediately. But she beamed up at him, so happy and…different than he'd ever seen her. Relaxed? Like any walls she'd kept up were gone, and she was certain she could break down his.

He couldn't let that happen.

"You could have all the information anyway, but I want you to know I'm *giving* it to you."

He stared at her, wondering how all this positivity and sweetness and acquiescence felt like little daggers being shoved into his heart.

So he left, while he had some semblance of sanity left.

Ines was in a marvelous mood.

Being home? Relaxing in a way the cabin just had never fully been.

Being able to immediately storm through all Alexandre's defenses and have him in her bed—and meeting room—that very night? Incredibly satisfying.

She had not expected to be getting through to Alexandre on what was only the first day of Operation Real Marriage, but she *had*. There were still mountains to climb, but they felt…scalable this morning.

She had an hour before her meeting with the doctors, so she went in search of Evelyne. She hadn't seen baby Gabriel since he'd been born.

She found both of them in the playroom. Evelyne was stretched out on the floor with the baby laid on a little mat connected to a kind of arch that had things dangling from it. Evelyne reached out and sent one spinning, and the baby on the mat kicked his legs and gurgled.

The boy had grown by such leaps and bounds in four months, Ines's heart gave a jerk. She'd missed so much. It was another wave of being happy to be home. Being happy to be part of this family. If there were things she had to fight for, so be it.

Her child would have a family. Not just a loving father, but an aunt and an uncle and a cousin—probably more than one. Her child would *never* be anyone's pawn or bargaining chip. And it wasn't just *her* who would make sure of that. It was the entire family.

"Good morning," Ines greeted.

Evelyne looked over her shoulder at Ines. She didn't smile. She didn't really do anything. Her expression remained a strange kind of neutral as she got to her feet and hefted Gabriel onto her hip.

"Gabri and I have an appointment," Evelyne said, and for the first time in their entire acquaintance the stiffness in her voice reminded Ines of Alexandre. Because usually Evelyne was bright and vibrant and…warm. Welcoming. No matter *what* was going on around them.

Now she walked past Ines without a second glance. Said nothing else. Ines watched her walk to the door and had the sickening realization something was not right.

"I… Are you angry with me?"

Evelyne didn't turn to face her. But she stood still. For a moment, the stiff posture reminded Ines so much of Alexandre she assumed Evelyne would simply walk out of the room. That she had messed something up and would constantly be met with the cold detachment of the people she cared for.

Instead, the woman slowly turned. Her expression

was grave. "You ran away, Ines. Without telling anyone. Not even me. You do not get to waltz back into our lives as though nothing happened."

Ines looked at her sister-in-law, who'd become a friend. But she was still Alexandre's sister. "I emailed you. If I'd told you what I planned before, you would have told him. And he would have stopped me. And..." She didn't know what would have happened then. Maybe it *would* have been better. But she could not go back and undo what was already done.

Evelyne said nothing to this.

Ines took a careful step forward. "He's...your brother. I wouldn't have blamed you for telling him. I know how much you feel like you *owe* him, so I couldn't tell you."

"You shouldn't have run away from him," Evelyne returned. "He doesn't deserve that."

Ines's heart gave another jerk, more painful this time. Something close to guilt, even though Evelyne did not know everything about their marriage. She might be Ines's friend, but Ines had always been careful not to make out Alexandre to be the bad guy or the ogre.

She did not want to do so now, but part of the entire past few months had been about realizing...

"What do *I* deserve?" Ines asked quietly.

Evelyne blinked once, clearly surprised by the question. And unsettled, because she offered no answers.

So Ines continued. "To haunt his life like a ghost and be happy with the crumbs he tosses my way on occasion? To never... I will not get into all of our private matters, but I deserve something too. I cannot simply exist to be whatever *he* wants without ever considering what *I* want. Not anymore."

Evelyne couldn't quite meet her gaze after that, but she didn't leave the room.

"Evelyne. Please. I cannot..." She had taken for granted that Evelyne would always be her friend simply because they both lived in the palace. The thought of losing that friendship...

"Please, don't be angry with me."

"It isn't that simple, Ines."

No. Nothing was that simple, and she had to be careful to remember that just because she'd found some happiness didn't mean simple was in the offing. She and Alexandre had a long way to go, and apparently she and Evelyne did as well.

But when Ines thought about it, she knew all her actions stemmed from something very—if not simple—straightforward. "I love your brother. Do you know that? Perhaps you don't. I don't think *he* knows it."

Evelyne frowned at her. "I didn't think—"

"I did not marry him for love, and God knows he didn't marry me for love, but you of all people know how good he is. How could I not fall in love with him over the past year?"

"Why would you run away from someone you love?" Evelyne asked. "It's not like if you stayed you would have hurt him."

It didn't surprise Ines that was Evelyne's only thought to running away—because Gabriel had run away from *her* for that reason months ago. But there were so many reasons to run.

"No, I would not have hurt him, but it hurt *me* to stay. Because he does not love me. Or at least, doesn't want to. Because I want so much more from him, and he is so unwilling to give it. But…this baby changes things." She put her hand over her stomach. "Running away doesn't work with a baby. So I'm back to deal with it, and him, and make him fall in love with me. And make him realize that doesn't have to cost him…his kingdom."

She hadn't realized what a tall order that was until she'd said it out loud. Sure, in her mind love should make it easy, but Alexandre—and Evelyne—were working against years and years of not having *any* love, any stability. They had spent their entire youth in survival mode.

Still, Evelyne had found Gabriel. Which meant *she'd* learned how to do more than survive, so Alexandre was capable of it too, wasn't he? Ines didn't know anything of Evelyne's and Gabriel's interior lives, except that Gabriel himself had been afraid to love, afraid of *himself.*

What was Alexandre afraid of?

Ines could only think there were too many things to count.

The baby reached out for Ines, and her heart tripped over itself. She had missed so much of his growth, and he was reaching out for her. But Evelyne would have to relinquish her hold. And she still hadn't said *anything* in reply.

But she let Ines take the baby. Still saying nothing. Just standing there, watching her.

So Ines looked down at Gabriel. "Aren't you handsome? And you'll have a cousin playmate soon enough."

Ines looked up at Evelyne. "They'll be friends *and* cousins, like Jonet and I. They'll have each other. What a gift for the both of them."

Evelyne's mouth curved, and she stepped forward, wrapping an arm around Ines holding Gabri. "Yes. How lucky they'll be."

Yes. Lucky. Ines liked the sound of that.

CHAPTER NINE

ALEXANDRE SAT BEHIND his desk and looked at the sociopath before him. General Vinyes was a problem, and while Alexandre had excelled at handling almost all the problems his father had left behind, this was one he hadn't quite worked out yet.

Vinyes was canny. It made him a more difficult foe than King Enzo, because while Vinyes was bloodthirsty and cruel, he did not fly off the handle. He had not quit in a rage when Alexandre had cut military spending. He had not voiced a true opposition to any of the peaceful measures Alexandre had enacted.

Vinyes went along, voicing *concerns*, but never disobeying a direct order. So Alexandre had no real reason to get rid of him, and keeping him on board had managed to appease some of the members of the council who might not have *liked* King Enzo but had liked the power supporting a dictator had given them.

So Alexandre was always on the lookout for *anything* that might make getting rid of Vinyes a just, acceptable choice. Just as he felt Vinyes was always on the lookout for a way to depose Alexandre if he made the slightest mistake Vinyes could leverage.

"I have heard rumors your wife has returned from her...*holiday*," Vinyes said.

Alexandre held himself very still. He did not like Vinyes mentioning *any* of the women in this palace. There was something about the way he spoke that always made it feel like a threat.

But Vinyes hadn't *acted* on anything that was or felt like a threat, leaving Alexandre with a frustrating impotent feeling.

Alexandre made sure his voice was devoid of any reaction before he spoke. "I'm not sure *holiday* is the appropriate word, as she maintained many of her duties while away."

Vinyes made a noncommittal kind of sound. "Highly unusual, that."

"I wanted Ines away from the stressors of the palace for a bit." Alexandre tried for a smile but wasn't sure he managed.

"No trouble, I hope?"

Alex held the general's gaze. Flat. Cold. "None." *Clear*. "Are we done here?"

"You have not given me an answer on the necessary training stipend."

"Yes, I have. Quite a few times, in fact. My answer remains the same. Your men do not need training on weapons Alis will not be purchasing. We are not a military power, as I have explained on numerous occasions as well. I understand you disagree with that, but it is my choice and my choice alone."

"Your people do not matter to you, Your Majesty?"

It was asked with such feigned concern Alexandre

wanted to rage. But he sat behind his desk and regarded the general with cool disdain. "I cannot fathom what this has to do with my people, Vinyes. They have been quite vocal in their support of my peaceful measures, since the petty wars my father tried to enact were detrimental to our safety, our standing in the world *and* our economic wellbeing."

"I do not know of any people happy to be left unprotected."

Alexandre wanted to rub his temples, where a dull pain pounded. He remained in his seat, behind his desk, looking at the general who had refused a seat so stood there in a military stance, stoic and commanding.

Except, he could stand there and look disapproving all he liked—Alexandre was in charge. Alexandre had every last say. Vinyes was nothing without Alexandre's approval. And the man clearly knew it.

"The fact I maintain you and an army is protection, General. I have considered being rid of you both altogether." Which he should have kept to himself, but he was *tired*. And he knew who to blame for that.

He would *not* be tired if he'd slept in his own bed last night. He would not be *tired* if his wife was following the perfect balance they'd created in the beginning of their marriage. Instead, she was making everything more difficult, and he was bound to make a mistake because of it.

You cannot allow mistakes.

"Get rid of me?" The general laughed, low and bitter. Bitter enough it put Alexandre on edge…and filled him with hope that the general would finally *break* and give Alex something to fire him over.

But the door swung open instead, distracting both Alex and the general.

"Alex, we need to discuss—" Ines appeared, then came up short as if surprised to find him with Vinyes.

"I beg your pardon. Your assistant wasn't at his desk, and I did not know you were in a meeting." But she didn't leave. She smiled regally at Vinyes. "Good afternoon, General."

"Good afternoon. It is so good to see you after such a…long time."

There was something about Vinyes looking at Ines that made Alex's blood *cold*. So his words were equally so. "It is customary, General, as I'm sure you are aware, to bow to one's queen on her arrival."

A muscle in Vinyes's jaw ticked, but he gave a perfunctory bow. "I apologize, Your Majesty."

"Of course," Ines said sweetly. "Manners aren't everyone's strength."

It was a subtle dig. Alexandre wasn't sure Vinyes even picked up on it, but Alex did. It made him want to laugh. He might have, but Ines wasn't leaving.

He should dismiss her. He *knew* he should. That was the right thing to do. The thing that would appease Vinyes, at least a little bit. Send the woman away so the men could continue their meeting.

"I think that will be all, General," Alex said instead. Because he'd damn well rather be around his confusing, confounding wife than spend another minute having the same pointless argument with Vinyes.

General Vinyes looked at him, temper straining in his eyes. "I wasn't finished discussing this training."

"I was," Alexandre replied.

The general looked from Alexandre to Ines, then said nothing—gave no bow or anything else that would be considered protocol *or* acceptable behavior—and stalked out, clearly angry.

Alexandre should do something about it. Smooth it over. Fix it.

He didn't.

Ines closed the door behind Vinyes. Then flipped the lock casually. But the sound of it echoed through the room. Perhaps through *him*.

"I hope I didn't interrupt something important," she said, crossing to where he sat.

But he could only think of the locked door, even as she came around the back of his chair and began to rub his shoulders. She dug her fingers into his tense muscles.

"You *are* stressed, aren't you?" she said, a slight censure in her tone. "What was he on about now?"

"Just another attempt at strengthening the army, which I refused."

"I understand there's no good way to dismiss him, but I so wish you could."

"As do I. It never occurred to me he'd last this long without some kind of outburst or attempt at revolution." His eyes closed, head bowing forward as her fingers did wonders to loosen the tension in his shoulders. But it wasn't just her hands on him. It was her understanding of the situation.

Evelyne and Gabriel were a little more bloodthirsty. They did not quite understand the full range of diplomacy needed to right the ship of Alis, and they had a more personal hatred of Vinyes since he'd wanted to marry Evelyne and had threatened Gabriel.

In an ideal world, Alexandre could simply sweep out anyone who had supported his father, anyone who had made threats to his friend or wanted his sister as some kind of possession. But life and kingship weren't that simple.

Ines understood this. Her role. His. The caution required in such situations. And her hands were doing magic at the tension in his neck. He even sighed.

"I truly did not mean to interrupt. I assumed the front desk being empty meant you were alone, and I wanted to let you know the doctor's appointment went well. All is as it should be with baby and myself. They want to do an anatomy scan next, but since it will tell us the gender, I want you to be there, so we'll need to arrange a time. We'll also need to work out how to announce it to the kingdom. My clothes are getting tighter at an alarming rate. I won't be able to hide it much longer."

Alex didn't stiffen, if only because her hands were doing wonders on his tense muscles. But the word *gender* prompted visions of a *child*. He had seen Gabri grow from tiny little *lump* to a slightly bigger lump with a burgeoning personality.

And in mere months, there would be another baby in the palace, existing, growing, living. Becoming a *person*.

His child. A child he would not allow to face any

of the challenges laid on Alex himself at a young age. Neither Gabri nor his own child would suffer under the weight of his duties. He would need to find some plan for this, some way to ensure…everything.

"But I'm glad to have cut that meeting short," Ines was saying. "You would have tied yourself into even tighter knots if it had gone on any longer." She made a tsking sound.

Her scent enveloped him, and he leaned into the vanilla notes of that instead of the baseline fear of thinking about *children*. He let himself sink into the way it felt for someone else to take care of the state of his tension. Rubbing, kneading, easing it away. Her thumbs pressed up the back of his neck, and some *noise* escaped him. Not quite a groan. Just simple pleasure.

She slid her arms over his shoulders, letting them dangle there over his chest. He could feel her breasts pressed to his back and her breath against his skin as she leaned her head close to brush a kiss across his cheek. "I locked the door," she whispered in his ear.

"I know." He reached back, pulled her in front of him. She smiled down at him, taking a seat on his desk, facing him. She wore a typical outfit for an afternoon of meetings—a blouse under a trim jacket that matched the color of her skirt—except instead of the usual style that hugged her hips, this one was looser. With enough give that he could push it up her thighs.

Which he did. Taking his time. Falling into this lull of relaxation she'd created for them. He pushed the fabric of the skirt up to her waist, then hooked his fingers in the waistband of her stockings, and she toed off her heels so they fell with a thump on the floor between them. She lifted so that he could pull the garment off.

It wasn't *exactly* like that morning all those months ago. He was too relaxed to feel anger and frustration. Desire pumped through him, but it was warm and sluggish instead of sharp claws of destroyed control.

That had been a break.

This was a yield.

How he'd thought of her here in his office. How he'd relived that day over and over, against his own will.

This would be compounding the mistake, to do it again.

Or just enjoying a mistake already made. He did not tolerate mistakes, but making them with her took his mind off impending fatherhood and all that lay on the other side of *that*.

Or he just wanted her, and it was like a drug so that nothing else mattered but her.

Still in his chair, he tugged her jacket off her shoulders, but not all the way off her arms. It held her there, a kind of handcuffs if she did not shrug her arms out of the sleeves.

She did not.

Desire pumped through him, drugging him into forgetting everything except her, this moment, the blood pounding in his own ears. He could not be a real man in any sense of the word. He had to be a king. He *knew* this, but it was like she took away all his brain power so that knowledge was gone completely and utterly and replaced with only desire.

He wrapped his hands around her wrists so she

couldn't even shrug out of the jacket, restricting her movement if she wanted to. He needed some control. Some ballast.

"This will count as my next appointment," he told her. Because that would make it okay. Acceptable. Not another mistake. Just a duty done.

She was completely at his mercy. She couldn't move if he didn't let her go. And this was not out of the bounds of their agreement. It was simply...a little spontaneous.

But her eyes held his. Calm and direct. "I'm afraid not. If you want me here and now, you can have me. But you will *also* make your next appointment. You don't get to substitute on a whim." Her mouth curved into a smug smile. "But you may add whenever you like."

He should argue with her. He should stop. He should refuse. Let her go.

This would not be an *addition*. She did not get to determine that.

Instead of arguing, he kissed her. Deep and wild and hungry, holding her arms still so she could do little more than kiss him back. She made greedy little noises, squirming there on his desk. He put his mouth to her neck, scraped his teeth down the taut tendons there. She moaned his name.

He wanted to remove her shirt, but that would require letting her go, and he didn't seem to know how, so he only used his mouth over the fabric, and bit gently just where he knew it would send her arching back, gasping in pleasure.

He felt nothing but an ache, a need, and she alone

could solve that. Which meant it was a problem *he* did not have to solve.

Finally, he released her hands—not that she moved. Because he needed more. To spread her legs wide. She still wore her underwear, but he didn't even bother to pull them down, just moved the offending fabric out of the way and set his mouth to her. He tasted her, as deep, wild and hungry as the kiss. She cried out—and if anyone was listening outside his door they might hear. They might know.

He didn't care. Not as he drove her to a blooming, shuddering climax with his tongue. Her hand fisted in his hair as an anchor.

He pulled her off the desk and into his lap. The chair was just big enough she could straddle him. For a moment, his gaze was hooked to the swell of her stomach, the tiny evidence of his child growing there.

His.

He itched to reach out and place his hands upon it, *feel* it, the life she grew inside of her, but there was a terrible ache inside of him—one he was afraid would never go away if he did so.

So he kept his hands to himself and looked up at her on his lap. Her cheeks were pink, her hair tousled now, and her hand worked on the enclosure of his pants quickly.

It took nothing at all, just a few tugs, a little rearranging and she was shuddering around him as he moved inside her. So responsive. So perfect. Like she'd been made for him instead of the curse he knew she had to be.

And though he had no time, he took it, building her

up again. And again. And again. Reveling in the sounds she made, the way she felt against him. It shouldn't be here, but *here* ceased to exist. There was only her. There was only the way he felt with her.

A man, not a king. Helpless and out of control and *hers*, not his country's. The relief of that was as staggering as she was.

"Alex, *please*." It was the *Alex*, her voice, the sheer perfection of everything she gave that had him finally giving over to his own release.

Then she simply melted into him. Their breathing ragged, but she didn't get up. Didn't remove herself. She held on to him, and he found himself holding on to her, sitting in his chair. When he had responsibilities and meetings and duties outside that door.

"What are you doing to me?" he heard himself rasp. He should not have said it, but he did not *understand*. He could not seem to fight the temptation she was. She gave too much, and how could he be who he needed to be if she kept showing him some inner part of himself that had no place in the reality of his life?

She pulled back, still in his lap. She framed his face with her small hands. Met his gaze. Looked so *earnest*. "Loving you."

It was as if she'd thrown ice water on him. He went from a sluggish, sated confusion to ice. He felt ill. Actually, physically ill. Something old and dark poked at him, but he shoved it away. Set her off him and got to his feet. He moved away from her and these horrible words.

He knew what love could do. To kings and queens. His parents had claimed love, but all it had ever done was destroy. Not just each other. Him. Evelyne. Perhaps some people could wield the weight of love, but not a king.

Not *him*.

"Alex."

Her voice was quiet. Plaintive. "No." He roughly righted the state of his pants and didn't dare look at her. They had not discussed…*love*. Whatever this was, whatever they did… She could not fool herself into that.

"Darling, what's the matter? I—"

"Enough," he said harshly. Her words echoed inside him like icy tendrils of something he refused to acknowledge. Love. *Darling*. Something old and sharp clawed through him. Something he didn't let take up space in his head. Ever. "Put yourself together and leave. At once."

"Alex."

"Go *away*, Ines."

"Why? What is *wrong*?" she demanded. But she didn't sound demanding. She sounded soft and worried.

He *hated it*. It was exploding inside of him, building and building, and what would he do if she did not *leave*? Fall apart himself? Impossible. "I said go away." He swept a hand across his desk, sending anything in its path crashing to the ground.

A terrible loss of control. *She* made him lose control. *She* made him someone else.

His blood is in you, Alex. Always in you. You must always fight it.

He would. No matter what. He would. But if throwing things got her to scurry out of this room, it was worth it.

* * *

Ines was shaken, and it wasn't the sex. That was becoming almost normal. The wildness and the joy that came with it. The way she'd found she could make him lose his famed control. She was almost used to the heady knowledge that *she* did something to *him*.

But the aftermath of today was different. There was no triumph. She'd never seen him look so… She didn't even have words for it. The way he'd dismissed her had not been cold or detached or even cruel. It had reminded her of a wounded animal roaring.

There had been a naked kind of hurt on his face that she neither understood nor knew how to soothe. He'd tossed the contents of his desk at the ground, not at her, but the out-of-character outburst still left her shaken to her core.

She stumbled out of his office, grateful that his assistant's desk was still empty. Because she was about to *cry*. Even as her body still ebbed with the echoes of a pleasure too big, too wonderful for even Alex's horrible reaction to stop.

She had known he wouldn't react *positively* to the idea of love, but she hadn't anticipated it…hurting him. She couldn't fathom it. No matter how she tried to make sense of any of that, it didn't make sense.

She blinked back tears as best she could, but some fell anyway. She'd mostly put herself back together, though she'd left her pantyhose behind. He wouldn't be pleased about that. But she needed to get to her rooms. Get herself together and figure out…

"Ines?"

Ines stopped in the hall. She hadn't expected anyone to be in the common living room they sometimes all had tea in together, but apparently Evelyne was in there and had seen her pass the door.

Ines pressed a palm to the wall, squeezing her eyes shut. She breathed in deep, then out. Quickly she wiped the tears from her cheeks then backtracked. She stepped into the room with a smile on her face.

Maybe it was brittle, but it was a smile. Apparently not good enough because Evelyne's expression quickly morphed into concern.

"Are you all right?" she asked.

Ines nodded, trying to swallow the lump in her throat. "Where's Gabri?"

"Napping. I'm trying to get some emails dealt with this morning, and it's horrible. Come. Distract me." She grinned at Ines.

Ines tried to look cheerful in return, but she knew she failed.

"You look…" Evelyne's gaze of confusion turned into a wrinkled nose "…rumpled."

"I—"

"No, that's okay. Don't tell me. I do *not* want to know." She waved it away with a laugh. "In the middle of the day, huh? What *are* you doing to my brother?"

Ines's lump grew bigger. *What are you doing to me?* he'd asked. Like he didn't know. Like he didn't want it. Like she'd caused him pain when she'd thought it was something good.

And the way he'd dismissed her…

Evelyne's expression went back to concern, she

reached out and took Ines's arm and led her to the couch, then nudged her into a sitting position. Evelyne lowered herself next to Ines.

"What is it?" she asked.

Ines shook her head. "I—I'm not even sure I know. It wasn't a fight." Because it wasn't. She hadn't fought back. Alex had reacted, and she had gone away like he'd ordered.

Just like she'd always done. Obeyed. She couldn't even be mad at herself though, because her heart felt bruised. Because he was scared and hurting, and Ines couldn't *understand*. And God knew he'd never tell her, but Evelyne...

Ines studied her sister-in-law. A woman who had grown up in this palace, with Alexandre her protector from their awful father. A woman who had fallen in love, married, had a child despite all that.

Evelyne wasn't *hurt* by Gabriel loving her. She'd *fought* for it. For him. It wasn't the same, but she'd grown up with Alex. Maybe she could make sense of this for Ines.

"Evelyne..." Ines knew Evelyne's loyalty would always be to Alexandre, but this wasn't about getting Evelyne on her side. It was about...understanding. She studied her sister-in-law's face. "Did it ever scare you to love Gabriel?"

Evelyne took a deep breath as if thinking that question through very carefully. "I suppose it did a little, but that wasn't really the predominant feeling. It was more relief. That love could exist." Her eyebrows drew together as she studied Ines's face. "What's going on, Ines?" she asked gently.

It was private. Alex would probably want this to remain private. Or at least rather that she discuss it with Jonet, not his *sister*. But Evelyne had to have *some* insight, didn't she? She knew her brother. She was married.

"I told Alex that I loved him, more or less. He did not react...well."

"Well, you've come to the right person," Evelyne said with a brightness that didn't quite read as genuine. "You should have seen Gabriel's horror at me loving him in the beginning."

Ines wanted to smile. It had worked out for Evelyne, but this was different. It wasn't fear, it was something deeper. Something more substantial. Hurt. *Hurt* to be loved? It made no sense.

"I don't understand why it would...hurt him so. Gabriel was not hurt that you loved him. He was afraid. Of himself. I think I could understand that in Alexandre, but this is *hurt*. You were not hurt by Gabriel finally admitting he loved you."

"No," Evelyne agreed. "But Alexandre and I are not the same. Never have been. Both in personality and in how we were raised. As much as I love him, I don't understand... the deeper level he keeps hidden."

"But you were raised by the same man, in the same place. You were both hurt by your father."

"Yes, but our lives were not the same. From *birth*. Starting out, he had five years with our mother. He remembers her. He won't talk about her much, except in vague, glowing terms, but that means he remembers her enough that it *hurts* him to. I know she can't be quite the saint Alexandre makes her out to be when he *does* mention her, but she was a good person, other people have told me that. So Alexandre had that mother's love and then lost it. That's different than never having it."

Ines supposed that was true. Not that one was easier or better, just that it would mark you differently. And he was marked by the way his mother had died, even if he didn't acknowledge that. Everything she had today was because he'd been so worried about Evelyne he'd lost control all those months ago.

"The thing is, Alexandre was the boy, the heir. I was…" Evelyne shrugged. "I'm not really sure what I was to my father, but it was different for Alexandre. And I think, looking back, Alex made sure I didn't know the depths of that difference. He never let on that my father might be harder on him than he was on me. Alex always wanted me to…"

Ines waited, but Evelyne was clearly struggling with what to say. Ines didn't think it was out of loyalty, though, so she waited.

"I don't know how to articulate this as well as I'd like, Ines, but I think he feels like, sometimes, we deserved the way Father treated us. Like we *should* be punished for something. I don't think it's a *conscious* thought. More like being brainwashed by Father. He knows Father was awful, wants to be *nothing* like him, but his mind was still affected by the things Father would have told him, taught him."

Ines pressed a hand to her chest where an ache centered, spread. "I can see that," she managed to say, without even crying, though it was a hard-won thing. Alex held so much on his shoulders. So much *responsibility*. That no doubt stemmed from some kind of guilt the horrible king had instilled on him.

Because she knew Alex had not loved or respected his father in any capacity. That he'd dedicated his life to being different, to changing Alis for the better was clear in everything he did. She'd assumed that meant that he'd rejected everything from King Enzo.

But maybe there were deeper wounds he didn't know how to reject. Still, Ines could not figure out how that could connect to her loving him being such a *blow*.

"That doesn't explain why me loving him would be something that *hurt* him though. Shouldn't it be something…positive? Even if he didn't feel the same. Love is a good thing."

Evelyne nodded. "I'm not sure I could explain it. I'm not sure I *know*. What I do know is that anything positive, loving anything or anyone in this palace, would have only ever made him a target to my father. Perhaps it's an old echo of that. Fear that it will be taken away?"

Ines sighed. It didn't seem that straightforward. That sensible. But maybe Evelyne knew better than she did.

"The thing is, I only ever saw Alexandre handle Father expertly. He knew how to calm him, distract him, sometimes even stop him. But that had to have come from a place of… By the time I was old enough to be truly aware of things, Alexandre was a pro at handling Father. But he wasn't born a pro, I can't imagine. Perhaps our mother taught him. Perhaps he learned all on his own."

The hard way, no doubt. Because Ines knew from her months of being married to Alex before King Enzo had died that Alex did not agree with Ines's assessment. He did not think he was a *pro* at handling Enzo. He had felt like he was always just barely hanging on, just barely escaping disaster for himself and everyone around him.

He'd been the most tense she'd ever seen him the day of their wedding, because Enzo had promised Evelyne to General Vinyes. Alex had blamed himself for that, for not seeing it coming. So no, he wasn't a pro in his own mind.

Evelyne smiled reassuringly. "That just means you need to be patient with him."

"Perhaps," Ines said, diplomatically because she did not think *patience* solved the hurt on his face. She did not know how to *wait* for something to change when it was clearly a deep-seated trauma.

Evelyne grabbed her hand. "Don't give up on him. He won't see it, wouldn't admit it if he did, but he needs you."

Ines let out a long slow breath. She wished she agreed, but she wondered if it was quite the opposite. If by loving him and having his child, she was making everything harder on him.

The ache in her chest settled deeper, tears battling it out again. She would do anything to make life easier on him, except... Except she was pregnant with his child. Their child was growing and would be here eventually. She could not sacrifice all their child might have for Alexandre's comfort or ease. No matter how she loved him.

Which meant she had to find *some* way to get through to him. She forced her mouth into a slight smile. "I won't give up on him," she told Evelyne reassuringly.

Now she just had to figure out a way to get *through* to him.

CHAPTER TEN

Alexandre knew he could ignore Ines's missive. He was not beholden to meet her for a walk whenever *she* wanted. Even her list had acknowledged that *he* was the one who determined the time.

But he had skipped lunch and dinner with her. He'd convinced himself it was for work. The work he'd neglected because *she* had upended his morning.

She needed to get it through her head that he was a king first, second and last.

He would tell her that now.

Outside the sun was low in the sky, the air getting cooler. The gardens were an explosion of blooms and chirping birds. He never took walks in the garden—who had the time? There had to be a reason for such things, and the last time he'd had a reason was when he'd been wooing Ines.

But now she was wooed. The end.

He thought of the way she'd recounted their first meetings. She *had* blurted out that she liked birds, in a kind of desperate rush. It had eased something inside of him. If *she* was nervous but willing to take on the mantle of his bride, then… Well, it couldn't be so bad, could it?

So he'd endeavored to make her feel better about it. And she had held on to that kindness as some kind of sign that he was good...

There is only good in you if you make it, Alex.
There is no good in you. I will make sure of it.

He wanted to press his hands to his temples and squeeze the old voices away with it. He had not thought of those early days in some time. Did not allow himself to remember, wallow.

And the only difference in his life between all these years of shoving that turmoil away and having it live in his damn head was *Ines*. He did not blame her for his weaknesses. That was hardly fair.

But he blamed her for existing. For somehow reaching into his psyche and bringing those turbulent times back to the forefront. When his parents had argued, violently and viciously.

Over him. Used him as a pawn. A weapon against each other. And love with it.

In so many ways he had been some kind of linchpin in their marriage. His existence had caused problems. His mother's love for him. His father's love for her. She had not wanted that second child, had not taken care of herself because no matter how much she'd loved Alexandre, she'd known children were the death of her marriage.

Sometimes he wanted to believe that he'd been so young he'd simply misunderstood the things his mother had told him. He'd confused things.

But he knew he hadn't. Love had been a bludgeon— and so he'd been used as one. And where had that gotten any of them? His mother dead. His country in turmoil. So many mistakes he now had to set to rights.

And Ines would dare claim she was *loving him*. Ines was now convinced she *loved* him? No. Something had to give.

Loving you is such a curse for us all, Alexandre. I am so sorry.

No, he would not go back there. His mother had died years and years ago. His father was dead. There was no use reliving the past. There was only the future—of Alis.

He walked through the garden, growing more and more irritated he couldn't find Ines, when her message through his assistant had said the north side of the garden. The side of the garden he avoided. Did Ines know that? How could she? He had certainly never told anyone what he avoided or why. He rarely even thought of it.

He stood at the fork in the walkway. In order to get to the northern section, he would need to take a left. He would need to face that which hurt.

Well, what else was new when it came to Ines? Always forcing him into hurts that were better left buried.

He could return to the palace, refuse to take part in this ridiculous intimacy ruse, but then she would run away again, and he wasn't sure what little hold on control he seemed to have could survive it. Particularly with Vinyes making comments about Ines's *holiday*.

Plus, it was necessary to prove to her *and* himself that he was stronger than what strange feelings worked their way between them. These few months of torture would be followed by getting his *life* back.

He was used to those kinds of bargains, wasn't he? Years of dancing around his father's threats and whims had made him well acquainted with a devil's bargain.

And he always won. Because here he was, the king. Alive and well and fixing Alis, one step at a time.

He walked along the path, knowing every step would lead him to where he did not wish to go. But when had he ever had any say in where he went? A good king was not beholden to his own whims. He was beholden to his *country*. This he had learned from watching his father only care for himself—his ego, his temper, his wants.

His *love*.

Alexandre would be the best king, which meant rejecting all those things. No matter how Ines tested this. No matter what she was up to being in this part of the gardens.

The burial ground for one.

His mother's grave was not in the Lidia family cemetery on the other side of the palace grounds—where generations of Lidia royalty including his father were buried in the shadow of a chapel. If any god truly sanctified such an institution, it would have certainly burned to ash at his father being buried on its grounds.

Instead, the chapel survived.

Mother had originally been given an elaborate mausoleum in the capital city's cemetery. Buried far away from the family and Alex himself.

Alexandre had argued against this, even as a child. He'd been slapped and locked in his room for two days for the *audacity* to demand something other than his father's plan. He'd then been dressed up and trotted out for the funeral at the city center, surrounded by strangers.

The building, the stone, the memorial had been meant to show off the king's wealth and power, but it had left Mother separated and alone. A symbol and nothing else.

Just like you.

Luckily, Alex had been ill and didn't remember much of the funeral itself except feeling outside himself. But he had carried that day, that betrayal with him all his life. And he had always vowed to fix it when he got the chance.

So one of the first things Alexandre had done once Enzo himself was buried was to quietly have his mother's body moved here—not to the chapel but to the gardens. Not that he ever visited. But he'd wanted her safe and protected, as he had not been able to make happen in real life. She was still alone here, but she wouldn't be forever. He and Evelyne's family would be buried here. And Evelyne came to visit. She even took Gabri sometimes.

Alexandre could not fathom why Evelyne would subject herself to such a morbid exercise, but maybe it was different for her since she did not remember Mother. She had no memories of her voice, her perfume, the way she had snuggled him into her bed and told him stories of all the good he would do. Be.

Better than your father. Because you have all my love, and he has none.

Alexandre pushed the memory away. These memories only lead to one place. The bitter, bloody end, and that simply would not do.

Ends were over. He had beginnings to work out.

He spotted Ines in the distance. At the foot of his mother's grave. She was kneeling in the grass, the light fading around her as there were many trees here to create shade.

So many emotions battered at his insides, he could not even find some anger amidst them to hold on to, to use as an anchor. Or armor.

He approached her like a man approaching his own death. "What are you doing here?" He had meant it to come out sounding like a clear-cut demand—not a rusty, unsteady plea.

"Thinking," Ines said. She began to get up, and he rushed to help her to her feet. He did not look at the stone or the flowers she'd laid across the grass.

He might see that old flash of her dead body. Bloody. Desecrated.

Because she had dared die on the king, and even in death he had used his fists to make it worse.

Ines did not look up at him, instead kept her gaze on the stone. Alexandre breathed through the sickness roiling around inside of him.

But it meant he was looking at Ines. She was wearing the same outfit she'd worn in his office earlier—and even though it had been *hours*, she still looked a bit rumpled and mussed. Not her usual put-together, elegant self. Her eyes were a bit red and puffy. Almost as if she'd been crying.

Luckily there were so many pains inside of him vying for purchase this one did not cut him off at the knees.

"Would you tell me about her?" Ines asked quietly.

"I hardly remember her," Alexandre lied.

"By all accounts she was wonderful. The antithesis to your father. I would like to know about that. My mother… Perhaps my mother was not always the way I know her. But for as long as I can remember she dulled everything with whatever substance she could find. And I think my father preferred it that way." She finally looked away from the stone, up at him. Her blue eyes a vivid blue—that the tears in them seemed to bring out. "I want a role model to look up to."

He did not know what this was. He understood she might be upset with him for his behavior in the office this morning, but what did that have to do with his mother? With their child?

"What do you remember of her?" she prodded. The tears, the emotion in her didn't seem to disrupt her determination.

"Very little."

She sighed heavily, and she sounded *tired*. "Alex."

Darling, what's the matter? She'd asked him that as though she could fix it. Everything that was the matter. But she would fix nothing. And neither would he if he leaned on her.

It would all end in blood and death and bludgeons needlessly used against each other.

"I do not wish to rehash my memories of the mother I lost, Ines," he said curtly. "Why are you pushing this?" Always pushing at the things he needed to stay locked away.

"I want to understand."

I don't understand you. She'd said that when he'd

brought her back here. When she'd kissed him outside her room after running away for *months*.

But he figured that was only fair, since he didn't understand her at all.

Except he wasn't poking into *her* pain. "You think you will find some…childhood trauma that you will—what? Fix?"

She shook her head sadly. "No, of course not."

"Then, I do not see the purpose of this."

"I can't want to understand you?"

"There is nothing to understand beyond the fact I am the king of Alis." He had truly believed she'd understood this. For almost a year she had, and he could not fathom what had changed. What he had done wrong for all of this to come crumbling around him.

Except he had done nothing, changed nothing. *She* had been the agent of all change. If she had not pushed for an annulment, if she had not run away, if she did not continue to push at him to behave differently than he knew he *should*—walks in gardens, spending the night in her bed, sex in his *office*—they would not be having these conversations. He would not be in *turmoil*.

"I know you wish that were true, but it isn't," Ines said quietly. "You can't *be* a crown, Alex. You are a man. A man with a wife and a child on the way."

"A queen and a prince or princess."

Her expression hardened at that. "We are not our titles. However you see yourself, you will not reduce me to a *title*. A *pawn*."

"Fine, but *I* am a title. I will always be. This is fact. Not a point to be argued."

She blew out a frustrated breath. Good. Better frustrated than soft. Better they argue about titles than his *mother*.

"Do you want our child to be raised the way you were?" she asked him.

He could see it so clearly. Standing in that doorway as his father pounded his fists into his mother's dead body, Evelyne crying down the hall as the nurses tended to a child without a mother.

But no one had tended to him, so he'd watched a nightmare.

"No," he rasped out. He did not want that for his child. Didn't she see he was trying to protect them *all* from that?

"I do not want them raised the way I was either. I want something different for our child. But we are responsible for building that, Alex."

"He or she is not the heir, so it will be different."

Her mouth tightened. "That is not what I meant, Alexandre. And you know it."

Perhaps he did. But he didn't care. It would not be his concern. She would raise the baby. His job as father was simply to guide the child in the ways of the palace. Because a king was a father to many—not just one.

Perhaps it was not *everything*, but it would be better than anything his father had ever done for him.

His gaze moved, without him fully realizing it, to the stone with his mother's name. And what had she done for him in those few years he'd had her? *If I didn't love you so much, everything would be different.*

His father sobbing over an already-dead woman he was desecrating with his *feelings*.

"I mean *love*, Alex," Ines said quietly, as if she could hear his memories echoing around him. Using that weapon when he was at his weakest. "Our child will be loved. And I will love *you*. It is what we all deserve."

Perhaps they did all deserve something so destructive, but he would not abide by it. Or her words. Or these memories.

Because he was the king, and nothing would be destroyed on his watch.

So he left her there.

And didn't look back.

Ines stayed in the encroaching dark. There was something peaceful about this spot. Or maybe she was tired of crying, and she was afraid if she went into her bedroom, she'd just end up sobbing until she fell asleep.

It was silly to feel this crushed. She could not expect to get through to a person like Alexandre in one or two conversations. It would take time. To get through to him, to get to the source of his pain, and even once she understood it he would need time to heal from whatever it was.

Could he heal? She gave a little derisive snort. She should be worried about getting through to him at *all*. Healing was so far off it shouldn't even be a consideration.

But they had a *child* to think about, and he still didn't really acknowledge that. Maybe she didn't either. Though she had symptoms, it still felt strangely not real. That a child should be growing inside of her.

And she still had months to accept the reality. To bring it on board. For *both* of them.

Trying to shake the disappointment and sadness and worry away, Ines made her way back to the palace. So she could not get through to him regarding his mother—which was no doubt at least *some* of his pain, which seemed to be brought on by the idea of *love*.

God knew Enzo had not loved his son. So the only love he could have gotten was from his mother. There had to be *something* there, but he rejected letting her in. Letting her know.

He rejected everything when it came to her. Except sex. And even that she thought he'd reject if he could. But the powerful attraction between them was just a little too much to resist. She'd once seen that as a positive sign.

Now she wondered.

Once in her bedroom, she did as she'd feared. Cried herself to sleep and woke up feeling exhausted and achy, a headache from all yesterday's tears drumming at her temples. She felt so poorly she didn't even bother to get ready for the day. She simply trudged into the sitting room in her pajamas where tea and breakfast waited. And Jonet. Which wasn't a great sign.

"Good morning," Jonet greeted her brightly. A sure sign something was very, *very* off.

"What is it?" Ines asked. She had no polish, no strength to be anything but straightforward today.

Jonet shifted in her seat. She poured Ines a cup of tea. She took her time speaking.

"I have gotten a memo from the king's assistant. The king has, uh, been required to travel into the city and attend an economic conference."

"And I am being told this because…?"

Jonet blinked, clearly surprised by the acid in Ines's tone. Ines might have been surprised too, but she was too tired to work up to conveying it.

"He will be staying in the city, and so he wanted you to know he would not be attending any meals or walks or appointments for a few days."

Ines wanted to laugh—bitterly—but she didn't have any energy for that either. "Of course," she said instead. She looked at the tea, then waved it away. "I'm going back to bed."

"Ines…"

But Ines simply walked away, back to her bedroom. The next few days passed in a kind of blur. Jonet kept Ines on track, but it was the first time since joining the royal family that Ines needed to be told what to do and prodded into doing it. Usually, she took all of her tasks quite seriously, but she couldn't seem to now.

Those who knew she was pregnant blamed that. Those who did not know whispered behind her back—about her long absence and now her detached behavior. Ines couldn't even bring herself to care. Because, funnily enough, she thought both sides were right. Part of this exhaustion and emotional turmoil was brought on by pregnancy and hormones and growing a child.

And part was just plain old heartbreak.

"Are you giving up on him?" Evelyne had asked her last night.

Ines hadn't known how to answer that. She did not want to give up on him. She did not know how to get through to him. It left her in a terrible kind of no-man's-land, just waiting for the blow to take her out.

The morning Alexandre was supposed to return—in time to go to her anatomy scan—Ines forced herself to get ready in a way she hadn't been doing lately. She made sure she looked elegant and put-together, as befitted a queen.

Alex had missed their meals and walks, but tonight would be their previously agreed-upon appointment night, and if he thought he was getting out of it...

Well, they would just see about that. Even if she didn't particularly *want* to have sex with him right now or sleep in the same bed or even see his obnoxious face. He wasn't getting out of this because of the bad mood that *he'd* put her in.

She held on to that little blaze of anger because it felt like *something*, when most of the past few days had felt like nothing. Just *gray*. She'd take anger over that.

But the ultrasound technician had arrived with her equipment, and the palace nurse had ushered Ines into the room that was set up for the scan to take place.

The technician gave her directions, and Ines followed them, settling herself on the bed. The technician was ready to start, but there was no sign of Alexandre.

"My husband is supposed to be here," Ines said, her confidence slipping. What if he just avoided her from here on out? What if he was calling her bluff—daring her to run away? What then?

The door swung open, and in strode the king.

"I apologize," Alexandre said, closing the door behind him. He didn't even glance at Ines. His apologies were for the technician. "You may proceed."

"Um, well, of course." The woman smiled down at

Ines reassuringly. "This is quite easy, I promise. You only need to relax, Your Majesty," she said kindly. "I'll be looking for a variety of things, but once I can confirm the sex of the baby, I'll let you know. Unless you were wanting to be surprised?"

"No," Alex said, his voice very regal. The one-word answer a command. "We will know the sex."

"Of course, sir," the technician murmured. She got to work, and Ines didn't look at Alexandre. She watched the screen as the woman made the occasional humming noise as she clicked on this or that, zoomed in, hit another button. Anxiety tightened in Ines's chest.

She glanced at Alexandre helplessly. He was frowning at the screen, his own expression one of tension. She wanted to reach out for his hand, but he was just absent. And had been late. And what was there to reach out for if he would always walk away from her?

"Everything is measuring just as it should. Heartbeat, size, et cetera, all in line with your current due date." She smiled down at Ines. "Congratulations, Your Majesties, a princess is on the way."

A girl. They were having a girl. Every feeling in Ines's body simply whooshed out of her. She felt boneless. Empty. *Terrified* and...somehow overjoyed all at the same time.

She looked at Alex, tears spilling over her cheeks. Happy tears, a joy she couldn't fully understand. A *girl*, a *princess*. Something about this tangible thing to hold on to felt real when so little else had.

Alexandre clearly did not agree. His expression was blank. He held his hands behind his back, just as he had when he'd entered. There was *nothing* in him that gave way to any kind of reaction to the news.

"I've sent the results to your medical team. You'll only need to go to your follow-up appointment in a few weeks, unless there are any concerns. They'll contact you. I'll leave you two alone to…celebrate." The woman's smile was tight but polite, and she curtsied to both of them before exiting the room.

Alexandre stood there in silence, and Ines still lay on the bed, tears drying on her cheeks.

A daughter. She was to have a daughter. Who would be a princess. Who would be Alex's daughter.

He seemed very unimpressed, and it made her sad and angry at the same time. *Better than nothing, right?* She wanted to believe that, but it all felt so awful.

Except… No. She wouldn't let him ruin this. They were to have a daughter.

"We will need to discuss names," she announced, finally pulling her shirt back down over the swell of her stomach.

"Names," Alex echoed.

Ines got off the bed. She stood to face him. He didn't look at her, which made her angry. "Yes, our child is a person who will need to be named, Alexandre. I can handle it on my own, but I thought the *king* might have an opinion."

He looked down at her now, a bit like she was a bug to be wiped off his shoe. He had *never* used that expression against her. It made her feel worse. Everything about him made her feel worse.

"I'm sure you will choose appropriately."

She stared at him, fury turning her mute for a good minute or two. He wasn't even going to make a suggestion? He was going to leave it to her?

Fine. *Good*, even. Because she was done with this. Done with *him*. Her daughter would not live like this, hoping for *something* from her father only to get *nothing*. Ines didn't know how to accomplish that just yet, but she'd find a way.

I am the storm.

"Just so you know, you do not need to attend any meals, walks or *appointments* today. I do not wish to see you or be anywhere near any *kings* at the moment. I will let you know when that changes."

And with that, she marched off.

CHAPTER ELEVEN

ALEXANDRE SAT AT his desk, trying to focus on his ever-growing to-do list. Instead, he kept thinking about Ines.

And a *princess*. A daughter. His. To protect.

He had protected Evelyne. Not perfectly, but from the *worst* of things. He still counted it as a partial failure, but this would be different. It had to be. He could protect his princess.

Your daughter.

He was an adult now. The king. He did not have to try to stop the whims of someone else, so she would be… She would be fine.

Names. Ines wanted him to have a say in a name, and he could barely wrap his mind around a *baby*. A girl. His.

All the ways he'd failed Evelyne felt bigger in his head now. Alex would never lay a hand on his daughter as Enzo had, but that didn't mean he would be *good* at this. He was a *king*, not a father. Didn't being a good father require him to be more than a title? He couldn't be.

He was a protector—of *all* in his kingdom, not someone to think of names and futures and…

A *daughter*. What was he supposed to do with this?

It felt like a terrible unfurling in his chest, painful with claws. It was hard to breathe. Impossible to think of anything beyond that staticky picture on the screen. It hadn't looked like much more than a blob to Alexandre, but the technician had confidently seen something.

A girl. *His* daughter.

Gabriel strode in unannounced, but Alex heard his assistant huffing and puffing from behind him. "We have a problem," Gabriel said seriously, ignoring the flustered assistant.

Alexandre wanted to rap his head on the desk. He had more problems than he could begin to count. Instead, he waved his assistant away. "Hold my calls until we're done," he told him.

The assistant frowned at Gabriel but did as he was told, leaving and closing the door behind him as he did.

"General Vinyes is up to something," Gabriel said once the door was closed.

Alexandre wanted to shout—something he rarely felt toward Gabriel, but he didn't have time for this nonsense. He had to figure out what to do with a *daughter*.

And a wife…who'd looked at him like he'd slapped her when he'd told her he trusted her to handle the names. He winced at the memory. Sometimes he behaved in ways he didn't understand how they hurt people—but he'd known this would hurt her.

He'd hurt her on purpose. And what did that make him? Not the man he claimed to be, certainly. Fists weren't the only way to hurt someone.

Still, he held his temper at Gabriel's interruption. By a thread. "This is hardly news. General Vinyes is always up to something. Do you have proof of said wrongdoing?"

"Not exactly. But I'm hearing whispers and—"

Alexandre pinched the bridge of his nose, hoping to pinch away the lick of temper with it. "I have told you there's nothing I can do about *rumors*, Gabriel. I need something real to be able to get rid of him for good without causing more problems than his existence does."

"It is a big *something*, Alexandre," Gabriel said seriously. "And it sounds credible enough I'm considering sending Evelyne and Gabri off to Italy and my parents until we sort out what the threat is and how we can stop it."

This poked through some of Alexandre's frustration. That *was* big. Gabriel might have no love lost for the general, but if he was worried enough to send Evelyne and Gabri away… "You think it is *that* dangerous?"

"There have been whispers of revolution. I haven't been able to get to the bottom of them yet. But everything I know points to Vinyes, and if he *is* at the source, it's more than possible. And it's more than dangerous."

"I need proof, Gabriel."

"Then I'll need your permission to do more than *listen*."

Alexandre knew how protective Gabriel was of Evelyne and Gabri, but he was not a man prone to exaggeration. If he thought it was this serious, it was. And as much as they might not see eye to eye on how to handle Vinyes, Alexandre trusted Gabriel. He would not behave outside of what Alexandre wished.

"You have my permission to get to the bottom of things, but all action must go through me."

Gabriel nodded. "Of course. You might consider sending Ines with Evelyne and Gabri as well."

"Why?"

"Revolutions have the tendency to get…bloody if not handled correctly."

Revolution. God, he hated that word. "Why…why would anyone revolt *now*?" There had been attempts against King Enzo here and there over the years, but Vinyes had ruthlessly stopped every one.

Those Alexandre had understood. Perhaps even rooted for from time to time, even if he himself would have ended up on one of their pikes. He couldn't blame those who hated his father's reign.

But him? He'd done everything to *solve* the problems his father had created. Maybe it was taking longer than some people liked. Maybe it wasn't *perfect*. But to revolt now when there was actually progress being made?

"Sometimes people love a cage, Alexandre," Gabriel said quietly. "Vinyes certainly knows how to make them believe they aren't in one. Most of the people are behind you. You know this, but it only takes a well-connected few to threaten that. A general is pretty damn well connected. A bloodthirsty one? Well, he doesn't need the will of the people. He only needs the might of a few, and access to a king."

It made more sense, honestly, that Vinyes was pretending to be a dutiful general who listened to his king while secretly planning some kind of revolution rather than just trying to keep his job, but it didn't make it any easier to hear.

What would Alexandre do if the general used his own army against him? Surely not all the soldiers would heed Vinyes's commands. Vinyes was no loved leader, but Gabriel was right. People loved a cage that felt like safety. And people would do a lot of things out of fear.

Fear. Ines. His *daughter*. Safety.

Here in this palace while someone planned revolution. No, that could not be. He had to protect them. Always.

"I cannot imagine Ines would want to go, but..." Well, she wasn't happy with *him*, was she? She didn't even want to see him. All the things on her *list*, all her determinations they should try to be a couple wiped away earlier.

She wanted nothing to do with him right now. *Kings*, she'd said. As though it was different. A person. A king. As though she was *disappointed* in him being a king when she'd known all along what she'd signed up for.

You do not have to be anyone but yourself with me.

But he *himself* could only be a king. The protector. The brick wall between chaos and pettiness and whims and personal vendettas and the right thing for the good of the people.

There were *not* two people inside of him—no matter what she thought. And maybe she'd finally realized it. She didn't want to be around him tonight. She understood. He was only a king.

An idea that he had held as a talisman that had gotten him through the worst. That *should* continue to but...

He shook that thought away and the discomfort with it. He should be happy he'd finally gotten through to her.

Why couldn't he feel anything but another weight around his heart?

"I will ensure she heads to safety as well," Alexandre managed. He would order it. Command it. And it didn't matter if she went willingly or with an argument. It would be done.

"Will she put up a fight? I'm preparing for your sister to. Evelyne will not want to go if we are planning on staying behind," Gabriel said.

"I am the king. I can hardly leave my kingdom."

"Yes, I know. And I will not leave you. I have connections with some of the soldiers. We will work to nip this in the bud before anything happens, but we do not want to risk anything. It will take some doing, but I don't think Evelyne could stand to be away from Gabri long enough to send just him to safety. I don't particularly love the idea, but..."

"But we must keep them safe. When is this to come to a head? Do you know?"

Gabriel shook his head. "Soon, I am led to believe. I will need to dig deeper to get a better idea, but I'd like Evelyne and Gabri off palace property by tomorrow."

Tomorrow. So soon.

Ines didn't want to see him right now. Maybe that would help their case. "It might go better if you or Evelyne discusses this with Ines."

Alexandre could not meet Gabriel's gaze. It would see too much. So he focused on some papers on his desk.

"What exactly is going on with you, Alex?"

Alex. A distinction this question was friend to friend, not lord to king.

"Nothing is going on. I am dealing with…impending revolutions and an impending child. It is a lot."

"It is, but these are not unexpected things. You've been preparing for both for months now, haven't you?"

Yes. He had known revolution was a possibility at the transfer of power, at the changes he'd instituted—though, he'd gotten a little complacent in thinking that dangerous between-time had passed.

And yes, the plan had originally been for Ines to have his child, but…

Not like this. "Ines has…developed ideas."

"Ideas?" Gabriel returned equitably. "Or feelings?"

Alex scraped a palm over his jaw. "She is simply confused. Perhaps…hormonal." He winced a little bit at that, because he knew both Ines and Evelyne would take great offense at that suggestion, and they'd be right to.

But he needed a reason that Ines claiming she loved him was something temporary. Something he could *fix*. Her loving him would only end in pain and suffering. That was what love did, in his experience.

Gabriel sighed gustily. "It's beneath even you to blame *feelings* on *hormones*, Alexandre. Ines has been a wonderful queen to you and—"

"And I am a king. I have an entire country's fate resting on what I choose. How I handle this revolution. I cannot be concerned about *feelings*. Hers. Mine. Anyone's."

Our child will be loved. And I will love you. It is what we all deserve.

A princess. A daughter.

Names.

"You are more than a king, Alex."

But Alexandre could not take that to heart. Certainly not *now*. Why could no one understand that?

Because they had never been tasked with this. *You cannot save me, Alex, so you will need to save them. Do not change course. Do not let anything in. Be better than him.*

She'd been dying. Right before his eyes. Nurses and the doctor tending to the newly born Evelyne. No one had noticed him sneaking in. No one had noticed...

You must save your sister. You are her and Alis's only hope. If I loved you less...

Alis's only hope. He had held that close his entire life. His one duty. His mother had wanted it of him, so it would be done. She had not gotten to live a long, happy life. She had been brutalized, living and dead, by a man's selfish whims and uncontrollable, unpredictable feelings.

This was all he had to offer her memory.

So he could only be a king. *Only*.

"If there is to be a revolution, I cannot be more or less than exactly that. I am the king. Period." This was the clearest truth he knew, and getting Ines out from underfoot would help him remember that.

He had made a promise to his dying mother. Nothing would get in his way of protecting Evelyne. Of protecting Alis. Certainly not his own wants. Feelings. Self.

"Not all that long ago, you interfered when I was

keeping my distance from Evelyne and my marriage," Gabriel said.

Alexandre managed to meet Gabriel's gaze now. "You were afraid of yourself. I am not afraid."

"Aren't you?"

Alexandre frowned at Gabriel. *Fear* was not what he felt. He was making decisions out of experience and determination. Not *fear* of hurt. "I would never hurt Ines. I am not worried about that."

"I know. But love has always terrified you. Even when it comes to Evelyne and me, you keep a careful distance. That is why you save people, saved us. So you don't have to deal with the love you feel. You can convince yourself the protecting is enough."

Alex did not have words for long ticking moments. Then he shook his head, because Gabriel didn't understand. For Gabriel, love could be life. A foundation. A country, a legacy did not rest on Gabriel's shoulders. So he could be more.

Alexandre was different. He was a king. He had a mission. And yes, he protected people, but that was because of the title he'd inherited.

Besides. "Love is little more than a weapon," Alexandre muttered.

"I think that means you're doing it wrong."

Alex knew Gabriel wouldn't understand. Gabriel and Evelyne were…different. They might have titles, but they didn't have to save a country. They didn't have to walk that tightrope.

Alex had made sure of it.

Things would be different if I loved you less. How often had his mother said that to him? Like this giant love was a gift—even though it had taken everything from her.

She loves you more. You took her from me. His father's words. He'd turned from the queen's dead, bloody body looking like a monster covered in that blood. Eyes wild. Because for all the evil inside King Enzo he had mourned when Mother died.

He'd pointed at Alexandre then. *You took her from me.*

Alex had run then. But just because he'd escaped that beating didn't mean more hadn't come. No, it had only meant that for the rest of his days Father had blamed Alexandre for the love lost between them. Evelyne for Mother's death. Alexandre for her lack of love.

Always blame. Never responsibility.

That was love.

So Alex had taken on every responsibility. Even his mother's death.

Alex had always felt if there hadn't been a *kingdom* in the way—power and titles—these things might have been surmountable, but the palace made everything soft, complex, *messy* insurmountable.

The people would always come first. Had to. It was his role or he was no better than his monster of a father. Or he would fail the mother who'd loved him most at the cost of everything, even her life.

"Talk to Ines," Alexandre ordered—and it was an order, king to lord, not friend or brother. "Or have Evelyne do it. But I want Ines to go with Evelyne. If she is difficult, I will command it. But Evelyne should be able to get through to her."

Gabriel's expression was disapproving, but he nodded with a somewhat sardonic bow of protocol before striding out of Alex's office.

Ines stared at her sister-in-law while her gut churned with worry. She held little Gabri in her lap, because the boy seemed to like it here, and there was some comfort in the sweet, warm baby in her arms. She would have one of these in a few months. A girl. A *princess*.

Could she hold strong and wait and hope the reality of a baby changed Alex's mind? Or would that hurt everyone? She shook her head. More pressing problems at hand right now.

"They really think there is to be a revolution?"

Evelyne nodded grimly. "Neither Gabriel nor Alexandre are ones to overreact. They want us to leave tomorrow morning, if possible." She got to her feet, began to pace. Not just worry. Temper flashed in her eyes. "Protecting the womenfolk," Evelyne said disgustedly. Then she stopped pacing, looked at her son in Ines's lap and sighed, softened. "The problem is I don't want to be separated from Gabri, and you *are* pregnant. A dangerous situation is no place for us right now, even if I won't admit it to Gabriel. Or Alexandre."

Alexandre. Just the thought of him made worry the secondary feeling in her chest. She was just so…angry. But it wasn't the kind of angry that had prompted her to leave the castle all those months ago. It was something different. More complicated.

Probably because of the child she carried, more than anything else. Ines had more to think about than herself, her own wants and frustrations with Alexandre. She had a child to think about.

And he didn't even want a say in her name? He saw himself more as a king than a father? She wanted to think he'd change his tune when the baby arrived, but she knew the depths of Alexandre's stubbornness.

He'd just avoid the both of them—his wife, his daughter. Out of sight, out of mind. He'd never actually have to deal with *love*. It made her somehow both sad and angry, compassionate and full of righteous blame.

But for right now, if there was to be danger, he wouldn't rest until she was out of the way. Maybe a different version of her would feel Evelyne's temper, but pregnant and angry and hurt—yes, hurt mostly—she did just want to be away.

Not that she wouldn't worry. No amount of anger and hurt could turn the love off. And revolution could only be dangerous. Particularly when the man she loved was the king—and would be the target of any revolution.

She felt sick to her stomach just considering it.

She put a hand to her belly in some hope that might still the nausea, but it only reminded her she had another life to concern herself with. Her baby.

"I don't necessarily mind leaving right now," Ines told Evelyne. "But I wouldn't feel right invading Gabriel's parents' home. Jonet and I can go—"

"Don't be ridiculous. Gabriel must stand by Alexandre's side because they are basically brothers, and he has the knowledge and connections to hopefully stop this in its tracks. So you and I must do the same. Stand by each other. Together. Jonet, too, of course. Anyone you like, really. But we aren't separating. We are family."

Family. Fierce and determined. Nothing about the kingdom or titles. "Why doesn't Alexandre feel that way?" she asked, then wished she hadn't when Evelyne looked at her with something too close to pity in her eyes.

"This is about more than us leaving, isn't it?"

Ines nodded. She refused to cry all over Evelyne, but it took effort. "We had the ultrasound this morning. Did he tell you?"

Evelyne's mouth firmed, clear irritation. "He did not."

"We are having a girl."

Evelyne sat with a thump, then wrapped her arms around Ines. "That's *wonderful*. I can't wait to buy something frilly and pink."

Ines wanted to laugh, but she was afraid it would come out like a sob.

"He said he trusted me to name her. As though he didn't even want a say. As though he doesn't even…"

Evelyne pulled back and her expression was conflicted. Between the truth and her love for her brother. "He does care, Ines. I know he does."

"I know he does too, but it is so deep down I do not know how to reach it. And I worry he'll just keep burying it and our child will only ever know…a king instead of a man. Instead of a father."

Evelyne took a deep breath and let it out. "He is nothing like—"

"I know, Evelyne. I wouldn't be here if I didn't know

that he's nothing like your father. He means well. I think that's what makes it worse. How do you get through to someone who thinks they're doing the right thing? Who is *trying* to do the best thing but is just so misguided?" She shook her head. It didn't matter. This wasn't about her marriage or even Alexandre right now. "Will they be…in danger if we leave them behind?"

"I hope not. But I think it's possible if Vinyes is behind this, which of course he is. Father had uprisings when I was little. I don't remember much of them because I didn't understand what was going on, but Vinyes always swept through and took care of any protests. So he would certainly know how to whip one up."

"I cannot understand why anyone would follow Vinyes. Alexandre has done everything he can to undo all your father's harsh policies. Why wouldn't he be celebrated?"

"Change is painful. And complicated. And not easy. Violence is an easy promise. At least, that's what Gabriel tells me. I kind of think these are all problems made up by men."

Ines snorted. She couldn't disagree. Though the words landed deeper than the problem of men and revolutions.

Change is painful. Yes, it was. Could she turn her back on Alex because he needed to change and he resisted because of all that pain?

"But leadership comes with risks, and so we must let our husbands take those risks, not because they are *men* but because they are the leaders. We are leaders in our own way, but not *this* way."

Ines studied her sister-in-law. "You are such a good princess, Evelyne."

Evelyne blinked once, as if surprised by the compliment. But then she shook it away. She reached out, stroked a finger over her son's cheek.

"You'll come with us, won't you? We can keep each other from having nervous breakdowns worrying about our husbands."

That was the worst part, Ines knew. Even when she was mad at Alexandre, even hurting and despairing and not knowing how to get through to him, she would love him. Worry over him.

So no, she could not run away like she had before. Not that she wouldn't go. But she deserved something. Her daughter deserved something. Maybe she couldn't get through to Alexandre, but she was going to keep fighting. She was not giving up.

"Yes, all right. I'll come. On one condition."

"What's that?"

Ines lifted her chin and met Evelyne's eager gaze. "Alexandre comes and asks me to leave himself."

Evelyne wrinkled her nose. "Oh dear."

Oh dear, indeed.

CHAPTER TWELVE

ALEXANDRE HAD TROUBLE concentrating on what still must be done because his mind was focused on revolution, on *protection*. But there were still the day-to-day responsibilities of running a kingdom, and Gabriel thought it best as if they went on like they weren't aware of any *whispers*, so Alexandre had to be in his office, acting normal.

Alexandre agreed with this plan, but it didn't make his day *easy*. Particularly when only a few hours after Gabriel had swept into his office unannounced and, against his assistant's wishes, Evelyne did the same.

"You and your husband seem to think my office is yours to enter and exit as you please," Alex said, waving his assistant off, because he would not kick Evelyne out no matter how much he wanted to.

That was the purview of his father, and Alexandre was a better man—even when his sister was being ridiculous.

Evelyne rolled her eyes. "You must go talk to Ines."

He turned away from her to the papers on his desk. It was not a shock Evelyne would stick her nose where it didn't belong, but he had no time or patience for it. "Why would I do that?"

"She's on the fence about leaving with me and Gabri. You need to talk to her, convince her she should."

"On the fence?" Of course. Why would Ines just make things *easy*? He couldn't understand what had *happened* to her. Nearly a year of obedience and—

He went a little cold at the word. *Obedience* felt… ugly. He didn't want her to be *obedient* necessarily. Just…easy. Just… She should *understand* his bidding and do it without it feeling like orders against her will, because he was doing the *right* thing. They should go back to the way things were when she always agreed with him, always understood he made good decisions.

Which was clearly a lie. He frowned at that realization. It wasn't that she'd changed. She'd just stopped pretending. Why had she pretended in the first place, though? Evelyne never did.

Because Evelyne knows she's safe with you, no matter what, and Ines had to learn that.

He didn't know where that thought came from. He wanted to reject it. But the conversation with Ines about when they'd first met, about how she'd come to believe he was *good*, was all too close to wave it away as easily as he might have.

He looked up at his sister, bowled over by the thought that…he had always tried to protect her and felt he'd always failed, because it hadn't been enough. She'd been abused anyway.

But was the simple act of trying enough?

Ridiculous.

"I am busy, Evelyne." And in a terrible, knotted pain that made it hard to get a full breath. But he kept his voice devoid of that. Detached. Cold. "Tell her to be reasonable."

"If there's anyone I shall tell to be reasonable, brother, it is *you*."

He glared at his sister, but he recognized that look in her eye. Stubborn. Period. He was in no mood for the stubborn whims of his little sister. Particularly if just her existence brought on startling realizations he didn't want.

"I have a revolution to stop, if you haven't heard. Perhaps the two of you could concern yourselves with *that*."

"You have a wife who loves you. I cannot begin to fathom how you've made a problem out of *that*."

Alexandre stiffened in spite of himself. What had Ines told her? Why was she bringing other people into it? "That is not your concern."

"My *God*, Alex. Be a man."

He straightened, temper stirring when he almost never let it stir with Evelyne because it was too much like Enzo. But *this* was a step too far, even for her. "I am a king," he reminded her. "*Your* king."

There was no room for a *man* in that equation. He'd learned that as a *child*. How had she not?

She looked wholly unimpressed by that. "You're an ass."

He stared at her in shock. Not that she was never rude to him, but it had been quite some time, and usually she wasn't taking someone else's side when she did it.

"An ass," she continued, using that offensive word once again, "who must *ask* his wife and the mother of his future child himself if he wishes her to leave him so he can fight a revolution alone," she continued, clearly not backing down.

Alexandre could blame Ines for this too, that Evelyne would stick her nose in this. Because if there was no Ines, Evelyne and Gabri would just be on their way to safety.

"I will not be fighting anything alone."

"No, my husband and the father of *my* child will stand beside you. Something Gabriel and I discussed. Together. Because we both love you and each other."

He did not have time for this. He did not *have* to do this. He was the king. Only his command mattered.

His breath caught when he realized…that way lay the way of his father.

But that did not mean he couldn't find—wouldn't find—his own way. He looked his sister in the eye and asked her very plainly, "Evelyne, what do you want from me?"

Evelyne's expression softened a little—a very little—but her words did not.

"I want you to go talk to your wife. Really talk to her. I thought I knew you so well, or that Gabriel and I did, but I don't understand. She *loves* you. Why would you run away from that? You're the best man any of us know. There's no reason not to enjoy love when it's offered."

Best. But it was a constant battle. Did no one understand how *hard* that was? To be better than his father, *best*—for his country and his family. And Ines…she was a threat to all of that. Love or not. Maybe especially with *love* involved.

If I loved you less…

Love was a weapon. A bludgeon. It was pain and

suffering and *selfish*. Love destroyed. He could not be those things and save his country. Hell, he could not even be those things and somehow save his wife from the revolution that now threatened.

And people expected him to talk to her. Face-to-face. When all that ever did was end in…confusion. He had no time or space for that, but what else was new?

"I will talk to her," Alexandre agreed because it would get Evelyne to leave and stop talking about… whatever this was.

It would be easy enough to go to Ines and tell her she must leave for her own safety. And the safety of the baby.

Girl. Princess.

Alexandre squeezed his eyes shut as Evelyne came over and gave him a hug. "I know you care for her too, Alex. I know you *could* love her if you let yourself. I may not be able to understand why you won't or can't, but I know what it is like to be in love and be loved. It can be scary and hard, but it is hardly an enemy."

Alexandre awkwardly patted his sister's shoulder until she released him. He said nothing because there was nothing to say.

He wasn't concerned about love being *scary* or *hard*, he was concerned about it being used as some kind of bludgeon. Not against *him*.

Against Ines.

Against their daughter.

He had seen one lifeless, bloody body in his life, and he would not witness another—literally or figuratively.

Love was the root of too many mistakes. The kind

Evelyne and Gabriel did not have to worry about because an entire country didn't rest on their shoulders.

And good for them. They should enjoy that. They should have all they'd built. But he could not.

He could not.

He held himself very still until Evelyne left, then finally allowed himself to sink into his chair. One minute, just *one minute*, to pull himself together. He raked his fingers through his hair as his breath seemed to clog in his lungs.

Had he condemned Ines to this fate when he'd married her? He supposed he had, and for the first time he realized how unfair that had been—because she did not understand. She did not see the world as he did.

Maybe when this was all over, revolution thwarted, he could explain it to her in a way that would make sense. In a way that could turn something to good for her.

For your daughter.

He didn't know why that kept poking at him. Any child of Ines's would be well cared for and loved, and perhaps she would be a princess, but not an heir with that kind of responsibility.

No, that would fall to Gabri.

Pressure tightened in Alexandre's chest. He did not wish this on his nephew. He did not wish this on…anyone. He had only ever been concerned with *his* role, but he would not live forever. Someday, this all would be someone else's mantle to bear.

That little baby.

Who will be loved by Gabriel and Evelyne, and it will be different. You will make it different.

But if he could make it different for Gabri…

He shook that fear, that concern, that possibility away. Everything would have to wait until this trouble was solved. Even that.

So he went in search of Ines, because that was a tangible. He would find her, tell her she must go. She must be safe. The end.

He found her in her bedroom. There was a suitcase on her bed, open but full. Alexandre frowned at it, then her. "You've packed."

"Yes," she agreed, putting a little bag on top of the neatly folded clothes. She didn't look at him.

"Then I don't... Why am I here if you've already agreed to go?" Had Evelyne misunderstood something? What a waste of—

"I haven't *agreed*, exactly," Ines returned equitably. "I thought it best to discuss it with you first."

Frustrated and not at all understanding her, he fell back on icy detachment. "You know my thoughts."

"You wish to send me away, yes, but I wanted to be certain it was for my safety, not for your convenience." She sat on the edge of the bed, all regal elegance, and met his gaze with a direct one of her own.

Convenience. Temper licked, but he could not let it win. Not today. Not with all this *love* talk in the air.

"Ideally, there is no violence," he said, a bit through gritted teeth but clearly nonetheless. "I think Gabriel and I can stop this before it becomes something, but on the off chance there *is* some kind of skirmish, the children should not be anywhere near it."

Would Gabri face this when he was king? No, Alexandre would solve all these problems before he had to pass them along. That was the purview of a *good* king, and he would be that—revolutions or no.

But he had to stop this dustup first, and he could not be thinking about any of the things the women in his life seemed determined to poke into.

"Then I will go."

"Why could you not have simply agreed with Evelyne and let me be?" he demanded.

She rose from her seat on the bed and crossed to him.

"I am so angry with you for so many reasons I can't even count them all." She moved to him then, reached out and put her hands on his forearms. "But I still love you, and I will miss you and worry for you. And I didn't want to leave without saying that. To your face." Her blue eyes were shiny and earnest.

He stepped back from her before he realized it would be viewed as some kind of retreat. There was no retreat here. He had to stand up to her.

"Why does that hurt you, Alex?" she asked, such *pain* in her voice. Which wasn't fair. He did not wish to cause her pain—she was causing it herself. If she would just do as he said, feel as he felt... *Understand.*

"Do not concern yourself with what you perceive as my *hurt*. If you are quite packed, I will take your suitcase down myself."

"Do you feel nothing for me?" she asked, her voice quiet, tight, hurt.

The question made such little sense he didn't know how to respond to it.

"I thought perhaps things had changed," she said, her voice still vibrating with emotion. "That the thought of losing me might have opened your eyes, hence that morning in your office. And then again when I returned. Was I wrong? Was it all about avoiding an annulment? For the crown? Is that all it ever was?"

He should tell her *yes*. He should form that word. It would be so easy, and everything would be all right. "I never promised you anything to do with *love*, Ines," he managed.

"No," she agreed, looking solemn and regal and perhaps a bit shattered. "Nor did I to you. But it's there."

It was too much. This insistence. The hurt in her eyes. He had not done this. He was not pushing this. *She* was. *She* was using love as a weapon, and this was why he would not engage. He would not love. He would not *harm*.

"I have had enough."

"What about what *I* have had?" she demanded, temper flashing.

"What *you* have had?" he repeated, frustration reaching its boiling point. Everything he did was for *her*, for his citizens. And she complained when she was the one who had dismantled all they'd built?

"You have *destroyed* me," he shot at her. "Does this make you happy?" he demanded. "Satisfied? This love you speak of has only ever been used against me like a weapon. You are not the first. I hope to God you are the last."

It was too much. He knew it was too much. A break. She was always causing a damn *break*.

She looked at him like he'd lost leave of his senses. If *only*.

"A weapon? Love isn't a weapon," she said, shaking

her head. "What would make you think… Your father didn't love you, Alexandre. The way he harmed you and Evelyne was never love."

She said this with such certainty, as if she worried he saw the warped version of his father's attention or, even worse, his father's abuse as love. "No. Never. He never loved *us*." But Enzo *had* loved.

And Alexandre had enjoyed an unwanted front row seat to what that meant. What kind of adversity it caused. The stress, the blows, the end. Violence and grief and destruction.

All for love.

"Your mother also loved you." She said it like a statement, but it felt like a question, and it stirred up too many things that needed to stay in the past. His mother *had* loved him. She had tried to save him. She had been good, wonderful. Everything he did was for her memory and for Evelyne.

He was the protector in the face of all the ways he'd failed as a boy.

He turned away from Ines. "I will not speak of her. I have made that clear. You must go. It is for your *own* good, but you are making me glad of it."

"She did love you, didn't she?"

Ines wouldn't give up. She wouldn't *see*. "More than anything, Ines," he said, exhausted clean through. "Why must you belabor this point?"

"If she loved you more than anything, and your father did not, I do not understand why you feel so… threatened by me loving you. By me wanting you to love our daughter. If you would explain anything to me, maybe I could understand."

He remained mute for a wide variety of reasons while she sat there looking at him, seeking answers he didn't have. Even if she deserved them.

"I am trying to understand, and I cannot," Ines said, quietly but with deep, haunting emotion in her voice. "I know you want to be nothing like Enzo. I don't think you *could* be anything like him, but this is not that. So what happened to you, Alex?"

Alex, Alex, Alex. Always *Alex* with her. Always poking under all the walls he'd needed to erect to be the perfect king. The *opposite* king to his father.

"Happened to me? Nothing. Don't you see? Nothing happened to *me*. My mother died because of *love*. My father used her dead body as a punching bag. Because of *love*. My father violated the trust of his citizens and his duty to them. Evelyne suffered abuses her entire childhood that I could not stop, but I stand before you, all in one piece."

Ines's eyes were wide and bright and full of tears. She looked pale. "Perhaps in one piece, Alex, but no less marked. No less…warped."

"You dare call me *warped*?" he demanded. The shock of the blows just kept coming. "Just because my father didn't love *me* doesn't mean he didn't *love*. Oh, he loved. My mother most of all. Until I was born and ruined everything. Because she did not have room for both of them, only me. And he blamed me for that. *She* blamed me for that."

If I loved you less, I could be what he wants, but I love you too much for that. How often had his mother whispered that to him, as if it were some mantra to save herself?

But it had only felt like blame.

It wasn't her fault. It wasn't. It was *his*.

If she loved you less, everything would be the way it was. There is no good in you or for you, I will make sure of it, so she never knows your love. How often had his father taken his rage on not getting exactly what he wanted on Alex—a punishment for love.

Love was Enzo's weapon. His bludgeon.

And his mother's excuse.

And Alexandre had built himself to be everything his father was not, but he loved in spite of himself...and he would never, ever use it against another.

The silence was heavy, throbbing, but it was Ines who broke it first.

"And you'd never wield a weapon your father did," she said, with such quiet surety he felt as though she'd used her own weapon to cut him open. But in all that pain, he found some semblance of nothingness. Detachment. A bit like watching his parents fight when he'd been but a boy.

Over *him*. And he'd learned the only way to survive it was to retreat within himself. Through the fights, the abuses, the blame, the death. Even watching Enzo beat his mother's body. He'd learned how to exist outside himself. So that reality couldn't touch him.

Ines had upended that skill for a while, but it was back because this hurt badly enough he needed it to be back to survive.

He turned to face her then. He felt nothing but ice

and was relieved. Because she understood, so maybe he could *survive*. "No. I will not. The car will take you and Evelyne and Gabri to the airport first thing in the morning. You will be ready." He did not pose it as a question.

She studied him, her hands clasped together over her heart as if she could feel his own pain radiating inside of her chest. She looked broken. Appalled.

But there were worse things in her eyes. Worse even than the tears. Something too close to pity to be considered anything but.

He was a *king*. He was not meant to be pitied.

"We can go back to the way things were." There were tears in her eyes, but they didn't fall. There was a shake in her voice, but each word came out clear. "I will make it all as easy on you as possible. I will go while you fight this threat, and when I came back, it can all go back to the way it was."

He had no words for this strange turnaround. No way to fight the shocking *pain* those words elicited, when he should feel nothing but relief. Or the calm detachment of disassociating.

"But I will love our daughter," she continued fiercely. "With all I am. And I will prove to you that it will not warp me. It will not be a weapon. Because what your father called love, and perhaps even your mother, was nothing more than *control*, Alexandre. And you of all people should know that. You are not your father, but you have certainly learned how to control the world around you. You do it for good, but that does not make it good."

He had no words. He couldn't even breathe. Was she

accusing him of being, if not as bad as his father, still not *better*?

"I love you," she said firmly, never looking away from him. "That's not a weapon. It's only a fact. It is only a *promise*."

But he felt stabbed clean all the same, as though it was nothing more than a dagger shoved into his heart.

"When you are ready to heal from these horrible things you saw and felt, I will be here." She pressed her palm to her stomach. "We will be here."

"I will never be ready." Because there was nothing to *heal* from. He had endured. Survived. He was a *king*, and his kingdom would remain in one piece no matter what he had to do in the coming days.

Men might need healing. King's were only the weight of their crown.

"Then, I guess we will all be miserable," she said, as though it was *he* who was the one damning them to that fate.

Before he could find words, or perhaps more likely before she could do anything else, someone cleared their throat behind them.

Alexandre looked back to find Gabriel standing somewhat awkwardly in the doorway.

"I apologize for the intrusion," Gabriel said, his expression apologetic, the set of his mouth grim. "We've moved up the timetable. The car is ready. I'd like everyone to get out now."

CHAPTER THIRTEEN

THINGS MOVED QUICKLY THEN. Ines might have sunk into a depressed grief, but the threat of danger had her heart beating heavily in her throat as Gabriel packed up the car and gave instructions to a driver Ines didn't recognize.

Because the man was some kind of security guard who worked for Gabriel and not the crown, so he could be trusted not to fall into any traps of revolution.

Gabriel then said his good-byes to wife and son. Ines knew it was a private moment, but she watched the embrace, the soft whispered words, the lingering kiss from Evelyne, the last tight squeeze of Gabri, and ached.

Where was her husband? What was he doing? Off somewhere believing that this was a weapon. Believing he could only be a king—not a man. Save his country while sweeping his wife and unborn daughter out of the way.

She wanted to be angrier than she was, but how could she be angry at a boy who'd seen and felt and endured such terrible, terrible things? Life had never taken him by the hand and taught him different.

Of course he was afraid of love.

But understanding him now solved nothing, because there were no magic answers in his trauma. She had no answers, no ideas, only a terrible kind of grief welling up inside her.

The women piled into the car, Jonet helping Evelyne strap Gabri into his car seat. Ines sat in the back of the car, pressed in between Jonet and Evelyne, as it pulled away. Evelyne was silently crying. Ines felt too much fear to cry, but she pulled the handkerchief she kept in her purse out and handed it to Evelyne, who wiped her eyes.

"Are we doing the right thing?" Ines managed to ask. Because it didn't *feel* right. It felt awful.

Evelyne's gaze was down at the sleeping Gabri in his carrier. "Yes." It was clear that *yes* was for her son, not for herself.

Ines put her hand over her stomach. *Yes, for you. Everything is for you. No weapons. No bludgeons. Only love. The good, soft kind. The real kind.*

They drove to the airport and got on one of Gabriel's private planes that would fly them to Italy and his parents' estate.

The truth was, Ines didn't know how to fight what Alexandre had said. He was wrong, but he wasn't. He was living based on an experience that had shaped him, and he didn't know how to believe there could be a different one.

Perhaps there was only time and dedication to the task of proving something to him, but when their daughter came into the world, would time and dedication only hurt her?

Ines *would* love Alexandre no matter what. It was not something that seemed to shrivel up and go away. It was like some necessary organ inside of her. There was no deciding it didn't exist, didn't serve some necessary function to life.

So she would try very hard to give him the life he wanted just as she'd told him. She wouldn't pressure him for more. She would try to abide by his policies and decisions.

But not at the cost of their child's happiness. That would be where she had to draw the line.

Ines worried that there was no way to make everyone happy or even content in this situation. She worried, as she'd told Alexandre, that they would all just spend their lives in misery if he didn't come around.

She rested her hand on her ever-expanding bump. *I will not let that be the case for you.*

She had to find some way…some way for that not to be her child's fate. She could live with her own misery, as long as this baby was happy, loved, satisfied.

Once in the air, Gabri awoke, and Evelyne had him cradled in the crook of her arm as she fed him a bottle. She gazed lovingly down at her son, and Ines could picture it, more and more every day. This life inside of her being a child in her arms. A child to care for.

It would change everything. She wanted to believe it would even change Alexandre, but she worried he was ruled by such *fear* it would only drive him further into this determination to protect.

Not anyone else. *He* thought he was protecting those he loved, but Ines could see it for what it really was now.

Protecting himself, from the pain he suffered as a

child. Protecting himself from confusion and control and cruelty disguised as love.

She ached for him because she too had suffered, but not in the same way. Not with such a mantle of responsibilities on his shoulders. She had been a pawn in her father's plans—but he'd never pretended it was about *love*. He'd never pretended much of anything. A child was to be the parents' tool.

She had learned love from her friendship with Jonet, seeing her aunt and uncle together, reading books where hope had more power than cruelty.

She rubbed her stomach. *You will never be my tool. You will be your own. Love will never be a weapon.*

"What did Alexandre say to make you amenable to coming?" Evelyne asked softly, interrupting Ines's distressing thoughts.

"Nothing." Ines laughed, and it wasn't bitter exactly, but it wasn't cheerful either. "I didn't want convincing so much as an opportunity to say good-bye face-to-face. So I told him I loved him and would miss him, and I wished he would tell me why that hurt him."

"Let me guess. He got very quiet and commanding."

Ines almost smiled at Evelyne's very correct guess. "For a time, but I must have worn him out. Or worry over this revolution did. He got a little angry and began telling me things..." Ines shook her head. "Heartbreaking things. About how he sees love. *A weapon*, he said. Because that is how your parents used it."

Evelyne frowned. "My father never loved anything but himself."

"Alexandre claims Enzo loved your mother. That it became a bone of contention between them. I do not think it was love, but they called it that, so Alexandre thinks it was that."

Evelyne was quiet contemplating that.

Ines realized Alex had not discussed what he felt for his sister, how she fit into his views of love. Someone to protect, yes, but he also loved Evelyne. How did he view that if not as a bludgeon?

"But…he loves me. And Gabriel," Evelyne said softly, coming to perhaps the same conclusions Ines was. "They are like true brothers. They know each other better than anyone."

Ines wondered if Gabriel knew what Alex had told her this afternoon. She very much doubted it. "I don't know. I don't know how he justifies it. I only know he told me love is a weapon."

"He said that to Gabriel too," Evelyne murmured. "Gabriel told him he was doing it wrong then."

Ines almost managed a smile. "Do you think he believed Gabriel?"

Evelyne sighed, looking down at Gabri again. "No."

No. There was just something too complicated and complex, and at least some of the change or healing or whatever it was had to come from Alex wanting those things.

Maybe she understood that his awful childhood *had* marked him, but she could hardly make sense of all the different ways. Besides, he was an expert compartmentalizer. Evelyne probably had her own little compartment in his mind, more about protection than love.

"How do I get through to him when he's spent over thirty years believing that love is a weapon? I just worry that I cannot."

Evelyne sighed, leaning back in her seat. Gabri finished his bottle, and Evelyne shifted him onto her chest, where she began to rub circles on his back until he burped. She made it look easy, but Ines knew she had been gone for those months of the adjustment to motherhood, so she could hardly assume Evelyne had easily and perfectly adjusted to her new role.

"I cannot speak for everyone, but I do know something about deep-seated issues. They *are* possible to overcome, and I think love is one of the best things to help accomplish that," Evelyne said. "But sometimes so is giving them what they deserve."

Ines knew that when Gabriel and Evelyne had been having their problems, Gabriel had determined he was a threat. Instead of fighting him on that, Evelyne had agreed with him and let him go—not because she actually agreed or wanted him to go, but because he had to come to terms with himself…himself.

Gabriel had come crawling back, though it had required a little interference from Ines and Alexandre. Not that Alex had wanted to interfere. But Ines had made her case, that it was Alex's duty to get through to his friend.

Alex had done an excellent job of setting up a situation in which Gabriel would have to face the truth about himself. Ines had looked back on that moment as a bit of a triumph. Moving in the right direction. He'd listened to her. Interfered in his friend's personal matters that involved love.

She'd thought change was in the offing, so how had they ended up here instead?

"I don't suppose Gabriel could create a ruse in order

to prove to Alexandre that love is no weapon?" Ines asked, somewhat miserably. Because she did not know how to fix childhood trauma.

Evelyne smiled wryly. "If he could think of one, I would have made him do it months ago. But this is…"

Different. Complicated. *Alexandre*—the king of Alis *and* being stubborn.

"I've done exactly what he wanted. I've run away. I've demanded he be a husband. I've given up. I feel like I've done it all. And he's still…" Well, he wasn't the same, was he? He'd broken down and told her the things that held him back. That was new. Maybe it was even progress?

But it was hard to see what the end result of progress would be when there was the ticking clock of this child, of the love *she* would need from her father.

Evelyne reached over with a free hand and squeezed Ines's arm. "He does love you, you know."

Ines let that settle inside her. Did he? Did she know that? "I think I do know that, but sometimes I worry I'm kidding myself. How do *you* know?"

Evelyne smiled, a little sadly. "He has spent his entire life trying to protect people, solve problems, undermine the bad in this country, all enacted by my father and General Vinyes—and then fix it once he had the chance. I have never seen him… You don't make sense to him. By which I mean that you are something good for him—as a man, not as a king. He doesn't know what to do with that. I think it is new for him, and so it feels like a threat."

"A threat. Yes. Perhaps he thinks of it as a…curse,

instead of a positive. What if he sees love only as that weapon? How could I ever be the one to show him otherwise if he uses that crown like a brick wall battlement between us?"

Evelyne clearly didn't know what to say to that. She opened her mouth, but no words came out.

Ines sighed deeply. "Yes, that is the problem."

Alexandre had been able to set aside what had happened in Ines's bedroom. It was easy when things were moving at a quick clip. When the danger Gabriel had been concerned about seemed to snowball.

Vinyes had disappeared, along with a small group of soldiers. No doubt planning some kind of...threat.

Gabriel had been talking to all the soldiers he knew and not coming up with much, until a young soldier—who could not have been in service for any more than a year—had asked for a meeting with the king.

The man, little more than a boy, stood before him now in his uniform, explaining what he knew of Vinyes's treason. Where Vinyes was hiding and the number of soldiers he'd taken with them.

"You're certain?" Gabriel asked after the young man had outlined General Vinyes's plan.

Alexandre looked at the young soldier—wide-eyed, a little pale, hands shaking. But he stood there before his king and Gabriel and nodded. "I'm certain. And I am certain it isn't *right*, Your Majesty."

"Your information is appreciated," Alexandre said, somewhat stiffly. "We can offer you a safe place to wait until we've dealt with the Vinyes threat, or you may go back to your post. No one besides the two of us will know what was said here today."

The boy straightened, chin jutted. The signs of nerves were gone now. "I will return to my post, sir."

Alexandre nodded. "Very well. Should you change your mind, you only need to contact Lord Marti in the same manner you did before."

The soldier bowed, then walked out of Alexandre's office. Alexandre stared at the door as Gabriel closed it again. Gabriel looked at him, waiting for instructions.

Alexandre felt…at a loss. He was not *surprised* the general had handpicked a group of soldiers to storm the palace and try to enact martial law. What surprised him was how little fury he felt. It wasn't a detached calm either.

It was a kind of…exhaustion at the games men played when they could simply have a damn discussion. Just like his father. They could never talk, strategize, decide. It always had to be action. Feeling. Emotional outbursts, really.

"It was true bravery on his part," Gabriel said, "to stand there and do something he knew might cause him harm but was right. For the kingdom."

Alexandre eyed Gabriel suspiciously. He didn't know what Gabriel was going for, but it felt…metaphorical. "Are you drawing some kind of parallel, Gabriel?"

"He will make an excellent general someday, with some experience under his belt. I'd keep an eye on that one for possible promotions. No doubt you'll have to do some reconfiguring of the army once this is all done," Gabriel returned, not answering Alexandre's question.

As though he wanted Alex to *sit* with the metaphor and figure it out himself.

Alex grunted.

"Was there some parallel you *think* I was trying to make?" Gabriel asked, settling himself into one of the chairs opposite Alexandre's desk. He was not relaxed, though he was clearly trying to appear it.

Having Vinyes's plan was a good start, but now they had to decide what to *do* with it.

"No."

"Ah. Perhaps you are just distracted," Gabriel said. "I admit to missing my wife and my son. You seem to be missing…someone yourself."

Did he miss Ines? She'd been gone all of a few hours. She should be arriving in Italy soon, and she was with Ines and Gabri and *safe*. Missing her would mean admitting…

It hardly mattered. This problem wasn't about their families. It was about Alis.

"It is no hardship to love your family, Alex. It is not so different from loving your country and wanting to do the right thing by them. It is not so different from being a king."

Alexandre sighed. Because if all it required was for him to be *king*, he would know exactly what to do and how to proceed. But to be a person within the title…

All he could seem to see were the shells his parents had turned into, on account of *love*.

Ines had called it control, not love, and maybe it was. Who was he to say? He'd been a boy.

Did semantics matter? What did it matter what it was called if the end result was the same?

That poked at him in ways that had nothing to do

with revolution and everything to do with Ines. If he didn't call it love. If he didn't call it control. If he just accepted these feelings and tried to—

Gabriel's phone chimed. He looked down at the screen. "They have arrived safely with my parents." He let out a slow breath, clearly one of relief. "My men are in place to keep an eye on the property. I cannot imagine Vinyes will trouble himself or his men with them, but we'll keep an eye out just the same."

Because there was danger. Real danger in front of them, and Alexandre had to determine what to do. About revolutions. About traitorous generals. And brave young soldiers ready to stand against them.

"I know what my father would do with Vinyes and the rest," Alexandre said. He'd send an army into Vinyes's hideout and slaughter them all. Without a second thought.

"Have them all killed?"

"Yes." It would be swift and efficient and end this issue, but Alexandre was aware of what all his father's violence had wrought—more violence, anger, division and festering distrust Alexandre still hadn't been able to climb out from under—clearly.

Alex wanted something else. Not just power. Not just might and whatever *he* wanted. Alex wanted a solid Alis not just for the present day but for the future. For Gabri, the future king. For all who lived here and came after.

For your wife. For your daughter.

"We could go that route," Gabriel said carefully. So carefully even Alexandre wasn't sure if that would be his recommended position or not.

So he met his friend's careful gaze. "You know I cannot."

"I know. You will want to do the opposite."

But what was the opposite of violence? Forgiveness? Peace? It couldn't be *that* easy. "Vinyes will no longer have his position. The soldiers that followed him will face some penalty, but heaping violence on violence solves nothing."

"True. The problem is the opposite of evil and violence isn't always goodness and peace, Alexandre. We cannot simply give leniency and hope it fixes itself." Gabriel spread his hands as if to encompass the entirety of the problem. "The safety of our families rests on a stronger response."

Stronger. What was strength in this situation? Alexandre found he didn't have an easy answer. That might have concerned him, but his father always found the easy answer. The violent, reactive answer.

So taking his time wasn't *wrong*. Reasoning this out, looking at different angles could only be right.

The problem was, one of the angles *had* to be chosen. He could not simply refuse to act. Gabriel was right. The safety of too many people rested on action.

"What do you want to do, Alex?" Gabriel asked.

Alex.

Yes, Alex the man. Not the king. A man who wanted what was best for the future. For his kingdom, his family… and maybe even himself.

Alex. When this was a *kingly* duty. Except he was also protecting his family. And thinking of his kingdom. His past, his father's legacy, his own. The soldiers who would stand for him and stand against him.

Maybe there was not *only* room for a king in this situation. Maybe there had to be room for…all the roles he played, all the versions of himself he inhabited. Maybe he finally had to be one and be unafraid that it might crumble everything.

"We know where they are now," Alex said, thinking it through. If this had happened a few months ago, his actions would have been clear and precise.

But he was starting to understand middle ground. Complex ideas of duty and goodness. He could not be his father, but the opposite of his father, as Gabriel had stated, was not automatically *goodness*.

Ines had pointed that out to him as well.

Alex wanted to be *good*. He wanted to be *correct*. A king had to be. A man made mistakes.

Except his father had only ever been a king—only cared about money and power and military might. Not his children. Not his legacy. He had been a crown—a cruel, violent, controlling one.

The opposite of that was a kind, peaceful, compassionate crown…which was not necessarily *good*. Better, but not…good.

So what was the answer? It seemed he had to come up with his own view of what that meant. That he had to be not the opposite of this father, but his own *man*.

Ines believed he was a good man. Not because he was a king or the opposite of his father, but because of how he'd treated her before they'd married. And after. Up to this rather conflicted point of a few months.

And still she loved him. How did it make sense?

"We could send soldiers in," Gabriel said. "Not to attack, but to arrest. But we would need to determine how to get a message to the soldiers who would support you and see if they are willing to storm in and arrest Vinyes and his men. This is almost certain to lead to violence, a fight."

Alex didn't want violence or a fight, but he also could not let this stand, so where did it leave him?

"No." The plan took shape in a strange way. Gabriel's words about the opposite of evil. Ines's words about love and standing true. "We cannot avoid violence at *all* costs, but we can mitigate it. I want a special team to arrest Vinyes—as quickly, quietly, and without violence as possible. Then I want the soldiers supporting him brought here. I would like to address them."

Gabriel's expression was unreadable. "That could be...dangerous. Even without a leader they might not feel beholden to our laws if they don't now."

"It could be dangerous, yes, but I need to know. What is it they're against? What does Vinyes offer them? This isn't about right and wrong. We all think we're right. It's about finding the best way forward, and we can only do that by discussing it."

Gabriel still didn't seem entirely sure, but Alex knew this was the right way forward. Not might. Not kingly disassociation.

Connection.

Just like Ines had given him.

CHAPTER FOURTEEN

When Ines woke the next morning, there was very little news. Evelyne had passed along Gabriel's assurances that everything was okay, a plan was in place, and ideally Vinyes would be arrested by nightfall.

Gabriel's parents were kind and attentive and did their best to take Evelyne's and Ines's minds off things. They arranged a picnic in their pretty vineyard while they took care of Gabri, and Jonet joined the two women and attempted to chatter about all matter of things that had nothing to do with Alis or revolutions.

Ines tried very hard to set aside her trepidation and enjoy the sunny day, the pleasant company. To think of it as a holiday instead of running away from *revolution*. Instead of worrying if she wouldn't even get the *chance* to stand by Alexandre. To get under all his walls, all his traumas.

The day passed with no news. Ines grew more tense, but she thought she hid it well. Evelyne on the other hand... Well, there was nothing hidden about her nerves, her worry, her anger.

After dinner, they sat in the pretty, cozy living room—Gabriel's parents and Jonet having retired to their own bedrooms. But Evelyne paced while Ines rocked Gabri, finding the rhythmic movement and the baby's warm weight soothing. Ines knew Evelyne was concerned because Gabriel hadn't sent an update, but no doubt arresting a general took some time and careful doing.

Or he's leading a successful overthrow and Alex is somewhere hurt and—

She squeezed her eyes shut, trying to shut out the anxiety loop of her own thoughts. It was pointless. There was nothing she could do from here. There'd be nothing she could do at the palace. This was military and such.

This was a *king's* duty. Not a man's.

The fact that she understood that distinction better now than she ever had before was painful. Not only because she understood, but in understanding she had no idea how to get through to him. How to convince him he deserved to be a *man* too. Not when so much rested on him being a king.

He thought love a weapon, and his title armor. How could she ever foment her own successful revolution against *that*?

Footsteps sounded quietly in the hall, and then a man appeared in the entryway.

Evelyne stopped her pacing, then in the next moment crossed the room at a jog and flung herself at Gabriel, who caught her and held on tight. They murmured words to each other, too soft for Ines to hear—but it was not a moment for her.

Ines stood—Gabri still in her arms, her heart in her throat.

There was no Alex with Gabriel.

"Everything is well," Gabriel said loud enough that Ines was able to hear this assurance. "Vinyes has been arrested. Alexandre is currently interviewing and figuring out punishments for those who followed him. Vinyes will remain in jail until his court-martial. With the evidence stacked against him, his punishment will no doubt be swift and just." Gabriel, still entwined with Evelyne, moved over to peer down at Gabri.

The baby wasn't asleep yet but was getting there, with drooping eyes. Still, Ines handed Gabri over to his father with a shaky smile. All was well. Alexandre was busy, but safe. Safe. That was all that mattered now.

Gabriel held Gabri close with one arm and Evelyne with the other. Safe. Everything all right.

Except Ines felt very, very alone.

She pressed a hand to her stomach, reminding herself she wasn't alone. Perhaps her child was not born yet, but the baby still needed her for right now to take care of herself. And soon to hold and nurture and *love*.

"We will spend the night here and return to Alis in the morning," Gabriel said.

"Will Alexandre be all right?" Evelyne managed to ask the question which Ines hadn't been able to find words for.

Gabriel nodded. "Vinyes did not have as many followers as he would have needed to truly enact his plan. He believed more would follow than did. Many he thought would follow stood with Alex instead."

Ines felt her knees go weak, but she locked them. Her husband *was* a good king. He deserved such loyalty. If only he could take that on board. His goodness, his strength, all grown in spite of what he'd been given. If only he could see how *amazing* he was.

Instead, he hid behind a crown.

Evelyne let go of Gabriel and squeezed Ines tight. "Let's get some rest. We'll get up very early and head back home."

Ines nodded and even managed to keep her smile in place as the small family left to go to their room. Ines found her way to hers. She dressed for bed, then simply lay down in the guest bed, her phone in her hand.

She stared at the screen. She could call him. She could reach out and take that step. She so wanted to, and yet the fear of hearing that clipped, detached tone of his had her staring at the phone in her hand until she fell asleep.

She awoke to the bustle of everyone getting ready to travel back to Alis. Gabriel and Evelyne were cheerful, though baby Gabri was grumpy—which gave Ines something to focus on. She helped Evelyne and Gabriel try to cheer him up in the car and on the plane ride back.

When they returned to the palace, Ines excused herself and went to her rooms immediately. As much as she was desperate to find Alex, to hold on to him as Evelyne had held on to Gabriel last night—just to assure herself he was alive and well—she knew she wasn't steady enough for any kind of rebuff.

So she settled into a warm bath and tried to wash away all the worry and stress and focus on what came next.

She couldn't *make* Alexandre believe in love. Perhaps with time she could, but the misery she'd spoken of before they'd left the palace wasn't something she could stand. She had spent her entire childhood unloved, unwanted. A pawn. Perhaps she'd even thought it her due.

Until this new life had taught her otherwise. But it hadn't changed her parents. It hadn't changed anyone. *She* couldn't. People had to change themselves.

Just as she had made the decision to change herself.

Perhaps she would always be a little miserable Alex could not believe in love, but she could hardly condemn her daughter to the same fate. But what other options were there? She was a queen. Their baby would be a princess. What would Ines do if not this?

For the first time she thought she fully understood why Alexandre had worked so hard to be only a crown. To eschew anything that was *more*. By marrying into the royal family, she had made everything so much more difficult.

Trying to be a person within a title was complicated, difficult, and had no easy, perfect answers.

Or maybe that was just life—for everyone. A title was just a more concrete inanimate thing to blame the complexity on.

When she got out of the bath, Ines considered simply putting pajamas on and spending the day in bed, but the day after an attempted revolution would no doubt require the queen's presence. So she dressed to be seen.

Maybe she was reluctant to see Alex face-to-face today, but she still supported him, and anyone who came into her orbit would know it. Once she was happy with her hair and makeup and had found a skirt with an elastic enough waistband to wear over her ever-expanding middle, she forced herself to leave her bedroom.

She came to an abrupt stop as she walked into the sitting room to find Jonet waiting for her. Jonet had her phone in one hand, a tablet in the other, a clear sign she was in assistant mode.

Nerves jittered in Ines's stomach.

"I have received a message from the king's assistant," Jonet said, her smile somewhat apologetic. "He has an announcement regarding your pregnancy he'd like sent out today, if you could approve it."

Approve...

Alexandre wanted her pregnancy announced *today*? After everything yesterday had been, he was thinking about this?

Jonet held out the tablet. Ines took it dutifully, read the short statement.

King Alexandre would like to share the happy news with all of Alis that he and his queen will be welcoming a child to the kingdom in the coming months.

Ines found herself frowning at the words. *Happy news?* He had yet to act particularly *happy*. Of course this statement wasn't about Alex. This was royal business. "Yes, that's fine," Ines said handing the tablet back to Jonet. "I think I'm just going to go back to—"

Jonet cleared her throat to cut her off. "The second part of the message was that the king would like to see you now."

A message through *assistants*. She didn't have the wherewithal for that. "I'm exhausted, Jonet." She had only slept in fits and starts, and she knew she would need strength, true strength, to deal with Alexandre. Especially if this was how he was summoning her.

"Yes, but his assistant did say it was an urgent matter. I can put him off—"

"No." She might as well get this over with. Alex wouldn't claim something urgent if it wasn't. "I'll go." Maybe she didn't know what to say, but if he had an urgent matter, then they would deal with that, and maybe she could get away with not knowing what to do for the time being.

She walked through the palace. It had changed in the months since King Enzo had died. Alexandre had allowed Evelyne and Ines carte blanche to redecorate whatever they saw fit, and they'd mutually decided to move away from austerity and military, while keeping the historical integrity of the castle.

So Ines walked down carpeted hallways, taking her time and enjoying the art on the walls—landscapes and royal portraits, instead of bloody war scenes.

And, okay, yes, she was stalling. She wanted to find some center of strength—like Alexandre always seemed to have. She wanted to put on her queenly mask, but she was afraid the moment she saw him she'd throw herself into his arms. Relief that he was okay.

She just didn't want to be pathetic. Not because she cared so much about herself, but she had to start thinking about what her daughter was going to see. Alex had been incredibly harmed by what he'd seen as a young boy. She wouldn't do the same to her child.

So that was her center of strength. "You," she murmured, spreading her hands over her belly as she finally made her way to Alex's office.

His assistant nodded at her approach. "You may go right in, Your Majesty."

"Thank you," she murmured. Nerves battled, reminding her of a time early on when she'd been so nervous to be alone with him. Nervous because she didn't know how to read him. Nervous because she thought he was ridiculously handsome. Nervous because she had been afraid one wrong move would ruin everything.

But he'd always made sure she knew she could not *ruin* things. At every step in their courtship, he'd always assured her she was exactly what he wanted, even if he hadn't chosen her.

Oh, how that had changed. Now he'd accused her of *destroying* him.

She tried to fan the little flicker of irritation. Anger would stand against him better than *nerves*. Anger was better than pathetic, desperate love.

Or was it? Perhaps anger was the weapon, the bludgeon.

That thought left her feeling hollowed out, bereft all over again. She stepped into his office not knowing how to be, because she so badly needed things from him he wasn't ready to give, and she wanted to punish and save him from that reality.

When had life gotten so damn messy?

He stood behind his desk, hands clasped behind his back. Tall. Severe. Just like the first time she'd met him. His dark eyes unreadable.

But she had seen them clouded with passion, direct with fury, lost, sad. She had seen every emotion in his eyes, no matter how hard he'd tried to hide them. So she wanted to rush over to him as Evelyne had done on Gabriel's arrival last night. She wanted to cry—at least that she could blame on hormones.

But she stood across from him, frozen to the spot because he surveyed her with that detached calm that left her feeling travel-frazzled even after her bath.

I am so glad to see you in one piece. I am so proud you handled this the way you did. Your country will love you because you are a good king, but I love you because you are a good man.

All words she might have tried to say if her throat wasn't so tight.

"Good morning, Ines. I am glad you are back."

She blinked. Those were not exactly the words she'd been expecting. They hadn't exactly left on happy terms, so it worried her that he was *glad* she was back. Had he come up with some horrible new plan that would crush her?

She cleared her throat. "I am glad to be back. Gabriel's parents were more than kind, but I prefer…" *Home.* Not just this place, but a place she knew he was. Safe and sound and *home.* "I have approved the pregnancy announcement."

"Excellent. It will go out at once."

Ines nodded, feeling little more than adrift. Why was she here? She wanted to scream that at him. And yet all she did was stand here, waiting for him to speak.

He picked up something from his desk. A little notepad. She could see he'd written some things in his blunt but elegant hand. He crossed to her and held it out.

"I have made you a list, Ines."

"A list…" He'd successfully stopped a revolution, and he had a *list* for her. A list when he'd told Jonet, or rather his assistant to Jonet, this was some *urgent* matter. She took the outstretched pad of paper, but she couldn't quite make herself look down at it.

She couldn't take her gaze off him when he was whole and in one piece and something was just off. Something she couldn't put her finger on.

"It is a list of things we must accomplish before the baby is born," he said regally, perhaps noticing she wasn't reading.

He was giving her a...to-do list. Perhaps to keep her busy and away from him? Maybe that was for the best. But she couldn't seem to look at it. Not when he was within reach. Not when...there was *something* in his eyes she didn't recognize, didn't think she'd ever seen.

It terrified her. What if this was it? The end of the line. He'd stopped a revolution and now he'd stop her.

No. He doesn't get to stop you loving him.

"I have also thought long and hard about it," he continued, though Ines had no idea what *it* referred to.

"There was a queen of Alis many generations ago named Phillipa. She was highly regarded as brave and intelligent, no small feat for a woman to be given any credit in that time period."

Ines stared at Alexandre, wondering if he was suffering from some sort of sleep deprivation, because why was he talking about old queens? A history lesson?

"It is history, family, but it is also a symbol," he continued, his gaze steady and serious, but something was lurking in their dark depths that Ines couldn't quite identify or understand.

"I believe it would be a nice name for a princess."

Princess. Ines's mouth dropped open. Something

cracked open inside of her. "You thought of...a name." Her eyes filled with tears, but she blinked them back. She didn't know what that meant.

"Before you cry, read the list, Ines." His voice was... soft. She could not remember his tone ever being quite so resonant like that before.

So she finally looked down at the list in her hand and began to read.

We will breakfast together every morning. If I must miss a breakfast, I will make it up at the other meals of the day, and if I must be away for the entire day, you may punish me accordingly.

Punish... This didn't make sense, so she kept reading.

There will be no more separate bedrooms. You will move into mine—you may adjust the decor accordingly.

But that seemed to mean... Ines shook her head. Maybe this was a very elaborate dream.

We will continue to walk together at least once a day, per your list.

Her...list. But they weren't doing that anymore. Did he think she would hold him to it? She wasn't sure she could. Except...he had a list. One with another line to it.

Once our baby is born, we will revisit our lists and adjust accordingly to ensure we are both happy.

"What...is this? What..." It read like everything she wanted. Like a marriage. Like *love*. But she didn't know how to absorb that. Maybe she was hallucinating.

"This is to be on top of your list, of course. Except we are getting rid of *appointments* since you will be in my—in *our* bedchamber."

She swallowed at the lump in her throat, finally worked

up the courage to look at him. Was he really offering... all this? She couldn't quite trust it. "What brought you to change your mind?"

He sighed, closing the distance between them. His hands were gentle on her face. His eyes direct, maybe a little sad. But sad was something new. It wasn't detached. It wasn't walls. It was simply true.

"It is not that I have changed my mind, Ines."

Fear scrambled through her. And anger. "Then what is it?" she demanded, even as a tear slipped over onto her cheek. He brushed it away with his thumb, his gaze never leaving hers.

"A change of *heart*," he said, very seriously, very gently.

She inhaled sharply, held her breath there, staring at him trying to believe this was...really happening.

"Brought on by...everything. You. Our child. Gabriel pointing out that being the opposite of my father is not exactly a guarantee of *goodness*, and you had said the same. I have to be my own man, driven by my own core principles, and that man cannot be ruled by the kind of fear my father employed. The kind of fear that turned love into control or a weapon or whatever it was."

She couldn't quite find the words. Her mind seemed to be struggling to catch up to whatever this was, while her body reveled in his hands on her face.

"I met with the soldiers who followed Vinyes. I listened to these men tell me why they followed the general over their duty. For many, it was out of fear, bitterness. Things born out of feeling unseen, uninvolved, unimportant. And I realized that as a king I could not solve this for them—the fear, certainly, but I could not fix the things in their lives that led them to these feelings, because these feelings were not about them as soldiers, but about them as men."

She did not know why anger welled up inside of her when he was finally breaking through his walls, finally *giving, compromising, believing*. The idea that she'd told him all this and he hadn't *listened* but some rebellious soldiers would get through to him absolutely infuriated her.

"Well, I'm glad facing your men got through to you where I could not. Perhaps they can keep you warm at night." She tried to turn away, but he held her in place.

"Ines." His voice was so gentle. Almost *amused*, and her hands curled into fists, tempted to punch him—not that it would do any damage.

But his gaze was still direct. His hands still gentle on her face. "None of this would have happened if you had not done the fighting for me first. I was able to see this for what it was because of *you*."

The lump in her throat was back. A softening waved through her with such vigor she was afraid of it and tried to maintain her anger. "So, what? You're *grateful*?"

"Yes, grateful. But much more importantly, I love you, Ines. Not as a weapon, but as simply a…feeling. That we get to decide how to wield."

Surely he didn't mean… "I don't understand," she croaked.

"Don't you? You're the one who has been trying to get through to me." He brushed at the tears that fell over her cheek.

"You're just…suddenly in love with me because you stopped a revolution?" she asked, her voice squeaky.

He shook his head. "I have been in love with you for a long time. I think I began to fully realize it when you told me I needed to interfere with Gabriel and Evelyne's problems. When you stood up to me and showed me who you were underneath your mask. I'm sorry it took longer for me to be brave enough to look under my own. I'm sorry it took palace turmoil to realize that dedicating myself to the crown and only the crown makes me no different than my father, not really."

"You are wholly different than him," Ines said fiercely. Because no matter how confused or afraid or happy she felt, this was simply a truth they all deserved to know, to believe. But especially him.

"Perhaps *different* isn't the right word. Perhaps the point is... I should stop measuring myself against what he was or wasn't and measure myself against who I want to be. And I want to be the best king I can be. But I also want to be a man. Your husband. Our child's father."

Her heart was beating so hard against her chest, maybe she wasn't actually hearing him. But he still held her, still looked deep into her eyes like this mattered. Like they mattered.

Like they *loved*.

"Are you sure?" she whispered.

"Yes." He spoke without hesitation. "I love you. I will not stop. I will make mistakes, but I will endeavor to fix them rather than..." He grimaced. "I will do my level best not to try and *control* them but instead deal with them. Because that is what my parents did not do. They hurt each other to control, not to love. What they felt I cannot say. I was a boy. But I know they did not handle themselves as they should. As I will endeavor to."

He shook his head, as if irritated with his own words. "No, that is not right. I don't want to be in opposition to them or the memory of them any longer. I want to build something myself. I want *us* to build something. No measuring sticks. Just us trying to do our best with this love. For our kingdom, for each other, for our family."

Ines absorbed those words, and in them she heard the promise of a future—not perfect, not healed. But the journey *toward* healing. The journey of life with highs and lows, peaks and valleys, but love through it all.

"I will want to get rid of that hideous comforter on your bed," she managed to say, though her throat was tight and her words came out raspy. "And those curtains are an atrocity."

He smiled, the curve of his mouth so rare, and so wholly for her. "If you are with me every night, you have free rein, my queen."

She gripped his wrists, his hands still on her face. She met that serious gaze with her own. "I *am* yours," she said fiercely, because she would be fierce about this. About love.

"And I am yours." One hand slid off her face, smoothed down over her stomach. "Both of yours."

EPILOGUE

King Alexandre Enzo Rodrigo Lidia worked very hard to be a good king. He served his people and endeavored to make the right decisions for his kingdom. He still tried to fix his father's mistakes as king. No matter what happened, he would always wish to leave this kingdom to Gabri much better than he found it.

But, regardless of the outcome, he did not measure himself against the poor choices of his father.

He measured his success as a king against the quality of life of his people—lowered poverty and crime. Better health and education outcomes. Peace.

When it came to being a man, Alex didn't think of his father at all. He worked equally as hard to be the kind of man deserving of a wife as loyal and strong and wise as Ines, and a daughter as bright and happy as Phillipa.

Balance was not always easy or possible, and it still was not comfortable to sometimes need to pour more into being king and sometimes needing to pour more into being husband or father. But life was perhaps not meant to be easy.

Life was meant to be love.

And the palace that had once been filled with violence and anger and the pathetic whims of a morally bankrupt man was now filled with that love—Gabriel continued to work as Alex's closest adviser while Ines and Evelyne worked together to head charitable organizations and movements within the kingdom. Gabri and Phillipa grew like weeds—and Evelyne was due to bring another baby into the royal family soon.

"Pada!"

Alex got up from his desk at the sound of his daughter running into the office. She could not seem to decide between *papa* or *dada*, so she called him a mix of both.

It never failed to make him smile. She rushed over to him, and he hefted Phillipa into his arms as she nestled her head into his shoulder. She had her mother's blue eyes and his black hair. He swept a hand over the flyaway of it now—it often came out of the bands Ines lovingly placed each morning.

His darling Phillipa was not displaying sweetness for the sake of being sweet this morning. She was becoming quite the master escape artist. Something Ines was telling him he needed to discourage.

Alex couldn't quite bring himself to do so. Not when she escaped Ines's or Evelyne's or Jonet's or the nanny's watchful eye and came for him. Every time.

"Of course," Ines said, sweeping into the room with narrowed eyes. "There you are."

Phillipa dug in deeper.

"Picking her up is a reward, Alex," Ines chastised, coming over to stand next to them. "You'll regret indulging her escapes when she is a teenager trying to do the same."

Alex made a noncommittal noise, drawing Ines into him with his free arm. He pressed a kiss to her hair. "Let us all escape. This afternoon." He was still not a particularly spontaneous man, but sometimes love swept through him and he wanted to indulge in it. Away from the palace and responsibilities. Just him and his family.

Ines raised a brow. "Don't you have meetings tomorrow?"

"They can be rescheduled."

"As lovely as that sounds, there is something we best determine before we travel anywhere."

Confused, since usually Ines rewarded him quite heartily for spontaneity, he frowned at her. "What's that?"

"I haven't quite been feeling myself the past few days, and it *is* possible..." She slid a hand over her stomach.

He frowned a little with worry. "We haven't been trying for very long." Considering how long it had taken with Phillipa, Alex had assumed it would be another long wait to bring another prince or princess into the world.

"Apparently with the second one it is quite common to come a little easier. It's possible it's nothing, but let's be sure before we make any escapes, hm?"

Alex nodded, pressed a kiss to her temple again. Phillipa was wriggling between them, but it was just about nap time so she didn't lodge any of her usual complaints about not having her parents' undivided attention. "You've already made an appointment?"

"Yes, I was on the phone setting up a test with the doctor when she managed her little magician's act." Ines reached out, skimmed a finger down Phillipa's cheek.

His family in his arms, all this love. All this hope for a future that he had thought impossible for a man like him. But here it was.

"I love you, my queen," he murmured.

Ines beamed at him. "I love you too, Alex."

* * * * *

Did King's Heir Ultimatum *sweep you off your feet? Then, you're sure to enjoy the first installment in the Babies for Royal Brides duet,* Secretly Pregnant Princess*!*

And why not explore these other stories by Lorraine Hall?

Princess Bride Swap
The Bride Wore Revenge
A Wedding Between Enemies
Pregnant, Stolen, Wed
Unwrapping His Forbidden Assistant

Available now!

Get up to 4 Free Books!

We'll send you 2 free books from each series you try PLUS a free Mystery Gift.

FREE Value Over **$25**

Both the **Harlequin Presents** and **Harlequin Medical Romance** series feature exciting stories of passion and drama.

YES! Please send me 2 FREE novels from Harlequin Presents or Harlequin Medical Romance and my FREE gift (gift is worth about $10 retail). After receiving them, if I don't wish to receive any more books, I can return the shipping statement marked "cancel." If I don't cancel, I will receive 6 brand-new larger-print novels every month and be billed just $7.19 each in the U.S. or $7.99 each in Canada, or 4 brand-new Harlequin Medical Romance Larger-Print books every month and be billed just $7.19 each in the U.S. or $7.99 each in Canada, a savings of 20% off the cover price. It's quite a bargain! Shipping and handling is just 50¢ per book in the U.S. and $1.25 per book in Canada.* I understand that accepting the 2 free books and gift places me under no obligation to buy anything. I can always return a shipment and cancel at any time. The free books and gift are mine to keep no matter what I decide.

Choose one:
- ☐ **Harlequin Presents Larger-Print** (176/376 BPA G36Y)
- ☐ **Harlequin Medical Romance** (171/371 BPA G36Y)
- ☐ **Or Try Both!** (176/376 & 171/371 BPA G36Z)

Name (please print)

Address   Apt. #

City   State/Province   Zip/Postal Code

Email: Please check this box ☐ if you would like to receive newsletters and promotional emails from Harlequin Enterprises ULC and its affiliates. You can unsubscribe anytime.

Mail to the **Harlequin Reader Service:**
IN U.S.A.: P.O. Box 1341, Buffalo, NY 14240-8531
IN CANADA: P.O. Box 603, Fort Erie, Ontario L2A 5X3

Want to explore our other series or interested in ebooks? Visit www.ReaderService.com or call 1-800-873-8635.

---

*Terms and prices subject to change without notice. Prices do not include sales taxes, which will be charged (if applicable) based on your state or country of residence. Canadian residents will be charged applicable taxes. Offer not valid in Quebec. This offer is limited to one order per household. Books received may not be as shown. Not valid for current subscribers to the Harlequin Presents or Harlequin Medical Romance series. All orders subject to approval. Credit or debit balances in a customer's account(s) may be offset by any other outstanding balance owed by or to the customer. Please allow 4 to 6 weeks for delivery. Offer available while quantities last.

Your Privacy—Your information is being collected by Harlequin Enterprises ULC, operating as Harlequin Reader Service. For a complete summary of the information we collect, how we use this information and to whom it is disclosed, please visit our privacy notice located at https://corporate.harlequin.com/privacy-notice. Notice to California Residents – Under California law, you have specific rights to control and access your data. For more information on these rights and how to exercise them, visit https://corporate.harlequin.com/california-privacy. For additional information for residents of other U.S. states that provide their residents with certain rights with respect to personal data, visit https://corporate.harlequin.com/other-state-residents-privacy-rights/